Jane Austen's

Emma

MODERN CRITICAL INTERPRETATIONS

Jane Austen's

Emma

Edited and with an Introduction by

Harold Bloom

Viva Books

New Delhi | Mumbai | Chennai | Kolkata | Bengaluru | Hyderabad | Kochi | Guwahati

First Indian Edition 2007
Reprinted 2011

VIVA BOOKS PRIVATE LIMITED

- 4737/23 Ansari Road, Daryaganj, New Delhi 110 002
  E-mail: vivadelhi@vivagroupindia.net, Tel. 42242200
- 76, Service Industries, Shirvane, Sector 1, Nerul, Navi Mumbai 400 706
  E-mail: vivamumbai@vivagroupindia.net, Tel. 27721273, 27721274
- Jamals Fazal Chambers, 26 Greams Road, Chennai 600 006
  E-mail: vivachennai@vivagroupindia.net, Tel. 28290304, 28294241
- B-103, Jindal Towers, 21/1A/3 Darga Road, Kolkata 700 017
  E-mail: vivakolkata@vivagroupindia.net, Tel. 22836381, 22816713
- 7, Sovereign Park Apartments, 56-58, K. R. Road, Basavanagudi, Bengaluru 560 004
  E-mail: vivabangalore@vivagroupindia.net, Tel. 26607409, 26607410
- 101-102 Mughal Marc Aptt., 3-4-637 to 641, Narayanguda, Hyderabad 500 029
  E-mail: vivahyderabad@vivagroupindia.net, Tel. 27564481, 27564482
- First Floor, Beevi Towers, SRM Road, Kaloor, Kochi 682 018, Kerala
  E-mail: vivakochi@vivagroupindia.net, Tel: 0484-2403055, 2403056
- 232, GNB Road, Beside UCO Bank, Silpukhuri, Guwahati 781 003
  E-mail: vivaguwahati@vivagroupindia.net, Tel: 0361-2666386

Published by arrangement with:

Facts on File, Inc.
132 West 31st Street
New York NY 10001
USA

ISBN : 978-81-309-1883-9

Published by Vinod Vasishtha for Viva Books Private Limited, 4737/23, Ansari Road, Daryaganj New Delhi - 110 002. Printed and bound by Anand Sons, Delhi - 110 092.

Contents

Editor's Note

This book brings together a representative selection of the most useful criticism devoted to Jane Austen's *Emma*, reprinted here in the chronological order of its original publication. I am grateful to Susan Laity for her wit, erudition, and judgment in helping to edit this volume.

The editor's introduction first considers the relation of Austen's ironies of the Protestant will to those of Samuel Richardson in his *Clarissa*, and then meditates upon the dialectics of the will in Emma Woodhouse, a true heroine in the line that moves between Clarissa Harlowe and the representations of women in the novels of E. M. Forster and Virginia Woolf.

Stuart M. Tave begins the chronological sequence of criticism with his investigation of Emma's imagination, an investigation ironically qualified by its Austenian sense that "in so many ways her imagination dulls her perceptions and it blunts her moral sensitivity." Tave's emphasis is complemented by John Hagan's in his study of *Emma*'s closure, with his nice insistence that Mr. Knightley's proposal owes more to passion than to reason, more to desire for the imaginative Emma than to recognition and approval of her moral growth.

In a subtle analysis of Austen's dialogue, Juliet McMaster shows how the ironic power of understatement invests *Emma* with a rare emotional intensity. From a different perspective, Julia Prewitt Brown observes that if the sensitive values of *Emma* "are available mainly to the intelligent," the benevolence of social cooperation becomes all the more necessary. Susan Morgan, in an admirably comprehensive reading, uncovers a parallel between *Emma* and Wordsworthian inwardness and "sense of harmony with men and nature."

Frank Churchill receives a sympathetic appreciation, as an incarnation of the comic spirit by John Peter Rumrich, who grants Frank's unsuitability for Emma yet is moved by the tinge of Dionysian revelry thus brought into an Austen novel. A more traditional Austenian approach is ventured in the exegesis of *Emma* as "a comedy of intimacy" by Jan Fergus, who praises Austen for engaging her readers' sympathies as intensely as their judgments.

Invoking the context of "gossip," Patricia Meyer Spacks finds in that "female" cosmos both a means for achieving selfhood and for evading patriarchal constriction. This book's final essay, by Joseph Litvak, shrewdly corrects some recent emphases of feminist literary criticism by showing that Austen is most subversive not so much in exemplifying Emma's interiority as a defense against patriarchal structures by female subjectivity "but in locating Emma in this potentially endless circuit of fiction, interpretation, and desire," a circuit that renders the relations between women and men even more dramatic and mutual.

Introduction

I

The oddest yet by no means inapt analogy to Jane Austen's art of representation is Shakespeare's. Oddest, because she is so careful of limits, as classical as Ben Jonson in that regard, and Shakespeare transcends all limits. Austen's humor, her mode of rhetorical irony, is not particularly Shakespearean, and yet her precision and accuracy of representation is. Like Shakespeare, she gives us figures, major and minor, utterly consistent each in her or his own mode of speech and being, and utterly different from one another. Her heroines have firm selves, each molded with an individuality that continues to suggest Austen's reserve of power, her potential for creating an endless diversity. To recur to the metaphor of oddness, the highly deliberate limitation of social scale in Austen seems a paradoxical theatre of mind in which so fecund a humanity could be fostered. Irony, the concern of most critics of Austen, seems more than a trope in her work, seems indeed to be the condition of her language, yet hardly accounts for the effect of moral and spiritual power that she so constantly conveys, however implicitly or obliquely.

Ian Watt, in his permanently useful *The Rise of the Novel*, portrays Austen as Fanny Burney's direct heir in the difficult art of combining the rival modes of Samuel Richardson and Henry Fielding. Like Burney, Austen is thus seen as following the Richardson of *Sir Charles Grandison*, in a "minute presentation of daily life," while emulating Fielding "in adopting a more detached attitude to her narrative material, and in evaluating it from a comic and objective point of view." Watt goes further when he points out that Austen tells her stories in a discreet variant of Fielding's manner "as a confessed author," though her ironical juxtapositions are made to appear not those of "an intrusive author but rather of some august and impersonal spirit of social and psychological understanding."

And yet, as Watt knows, Austen truly is the daughter of Richardson, and not of Fielding, just as she is the ancestor of George Eliot and Henry James rather than of Dickens and Thackeray. Her inwardness is an ironic revision of Richardson's extraordinary conversion of English Protestant sensibility into the figure of Clarissa Harlowe, and her own moral and spiritual concerns fuse in the crucial need of her heroines to sustain their individual integrities, a need so intense that it compels them to fall into those errors about life that are necessary for life (to adopt a Nietzschean formulation). In this too they follow, though in a comic register, the pattern of their tragic precursor, the magnificent but sublimely flawed Clarissa Harlowe.

Richardson's *Clarissa*, perhaps still the longest novel in the language, seems to me also still the greatest, despite the achievements of Austen, Dickens, George Eliot, Henry James, and Joyce. Austen's Elizabeth Bennet and Emma Woodhouse, Eliot's Dorothea Brooke and Gwendolen Harleth, James's Isabel Archer and Milly Theale—though all these are Clarissa Harlowe's direct descendants, they are not proportioned to her more sublime scale. David Copperfield and Leopold Bloom have her completeness; indeed Joyce's Bloom may be the most complete representation of a human being in all of literature. But they belong to the secular age; Clarissa Harlowe is poised upon the threshold that leads from the Protestant religion to a purely secular sainthood.

C. S. Lewis, who read Milton as though that fiercest of Protestant temperaments had been an orthodox Anglican, also seems to have read Jane Austen by listening for her echoings of the New Testament. Quite explicitly, Lewis named Austen as the daughter of Dr. Samuel Johnson, greatest of literary critics, and rigorous Christian moralist:

> I feel . . . sure that she is the daughter of Dr. Johnson: she inherits his commonsense, his morality, even much of his style.

The Johnson of *Rasselas* and of *The Rambler*, surely the essential Johnson, is something of a classical ironist; but we do not read Johnson for his ironies or for his dramatic representations of fictive selves. Rather, we read him as we read Koheleth; he writes wisdom literature. That Jane Austen is a wise writer is indisputable, but we do not read *Pride and Prejudice* as though it were Ecclesiastes. Doubtless, Austen's religious ideas were as profound as Samuel Richardson's were shallow, but *Emma* and *Clarissa* are Protestant novels without being in any way religious. What is most original about the representation of Clarissa

Harlowe is the magnificent intensity of her slowly described dying, which goes on for about the last third of Richardson's vast novel, in a Puritan ritual that celebrates the preternatural strength of her will. For that is Richardson's sublime concern: the self-reliant apotheosis of the Protestant will. What is tragedy in *Clarissa* becomes serious or moral comedy in *Pride and Prejudice* and *Emma*, and something just the other side of comedy in *Mansfield Park* and *Persuasion*.

II

Sir Walter Scott, reviewing *Emma* in 1815, rather strangely compared Jane Austen to the masters of the Flemish school of painting, presumably because of her precision in representing her characters. The strangeness results from Scott's not seeing how English Austen was, though the Scots perspective may have entered into his estimate. To me, as an American critic, *Emma* seems the most English of English novels and beyond question one of the very best. More than *Pride and Prejudice*, it is Austen's masterpiece, the largest triumph of her vigorous art. Her least accurate prophecy as to the fate of her fictions concerned *Emma*, whose heroine, she thought, "no one but myself will much like."

Aside from much else, Emma is immensely likable because she is so extraordinarily imaginative, dangerous and misguided as her imagination frequently must appear to others and finally to herself. On the scale of being, Emma constitutes an answer to the immemorial questions of the Sublime: More? Equal to? Or less than? Like Clarissa Harlowe before her and the strongest heroines of George Eliot and Henry James after her, Emma Woodhouse has a heroic will, and like them she risks identifying her will with her imagination. Socially considered, such identification is catastrophic, since the Protestant will has a tendency to bestow a ranking upon other selves, and such ranking may turn out to be a personal phantasmagoria. G. Armour Craig rather finely remarked that "society in *Emma* is not a ladder. It is a web of imputations that link feelings and conduct." Yet Emma herself, expansionist rather than reductionist in temperament, imputes more fiercely and freely than the web can sustain, and she threatens always, until she is enlightened, to dissolve the societal links, in and for others, that might allow some stability between feelings and conduct.

Armour Craig usefully added that "*Emma* does not justify its heroine nor does it deride her." Rather it treats her with ironic love (not loving irony). Emma Woodhouse is dear to Jane Austen because her errors are profoundly imaginative and rise from the will's passion for autonomy of vision. The splendid Jane Fairfax is easier to admire, but I cannot agree with Wayne Booth's awarding the honors to her over Emma, though I admire the subtle balance of his formulation:

> Jane is superior to Emma in most respects except the stroke of good fortune that made Emma the heroine of the book. In matters of taste and ability, of head and of heart, she is Emma's superior.

Taste, ability, head, and heart are a formidable fourfold; the imagination and the will, working together, are an even more formidable twofold and clearly may have their energies diverted to error and to mischief. Jane Fairfax is certainly more *amiable* even than Emma Woodhouse, but she is considerably less interesting. It is Emma who is meant to charm us and who does charm us. Austen is not writing a tragedy of the will, like *Paradise Lost*, but a great comedy of the will, and her heroine must incarnate the full potential of the will, however misused for a time. Having rather too much her own way is certainly one of Emma's powers, and she does have a disposition to think a little too well of herself. When Austen says that these were "the real evils indeed of Emma's situation," we read "evils" as lightly as the author will let us, which is lightly enough.

Can we account for the qualities in Emma Woodhouse that make her worthy of comparison with George Eliot's Gwendolen Harleth and Henry James's Isabel Archer? The pure comedy of her context seems world enough for her; she evidently is not the heiress of all the ages. We are persuaded, by Austen's superb craft, that marriage to Mr. Knightley will more than suffice to fulfill totally the now perfectly amiable Emma. Or are we? It is James's genius to suggest that while Osmond's "beautiful mind" was a prison of the spirit for Isabel, no proper husband could exist anyway, since neither Touchett nor Goodwood is exactly a true match for her. Do we, presumably against Austen's promptings, not find Mr. Knightley something of a confinement also, benign and wise though he be?

I suspect that the heroine of the Protestant will, from Richardson's Clarissa Harlowe through to Virginia Woolf's Clarissa Dalloway, can never find fit match because wills do not marry. The allegory or tragic irony of this dilemma is written large in *Clarissa*, since Lovelace, in strength of will and splendor of being, actually would have been the true husband for Clarissa (as he well knows) had he not been a moral squalor. His death-cry ("Let this expiate!") expiates nothing, and helps establish the long tradition of the Anglo-American novel in which the heroines of the will are fated to suffer either overt calamities or else happy unions with such good if unexciting men as Mr. Knightley or Will Ladislaw in *Middlemarch*. When George Eliot is reduced to having the fascinating Gwendolen Harleth fall hopelessly in love with the prince of prigs, Daniel Deronda, we sigh and resign ourselves to the sorrows of fictive overdetermination. Lovelace or Daniel Deronda? I myself do not know a high-spirited woman who would not prefer the first, though not for a husband!

Emma is replete with grand comic epiphanies, of which my favorite comes in volume 3, chapter 11, when Emma receives the grave shock of Harriet's disclosure that Mr. Knightley is the object of Harriet's hopeful affections:

> When Harriet had closed her evidence, she appealed to her dear Miss Woodhouse, to say whether she had not good ground for hope.
>
> "I never should have presumed to think of it at first," said she, "but for you. You told me to observe him carefully, and let his behavior be the rule of mine—and so I have. But now I seem to feel that I may deserve him; and that if he does choose me, it will not be any thing so very wonderful."
>
> The bitter feelings occasioned by this speech, the many bitter feelings, made the utmost exertion necessary on Emma's side to enable her to say in reply,
>
> "Harriet, I will only venture to declare, that Mr. Knightley is the last man in the world, who would intentionally give any woman the idea of his feeling for her more than he really does."
>
> Harriet seemed ready to worship her friend for a sentence so satisfactory; and Emma was only saved from raptures and fondness, which at the moment would have been dreadful penance, by the sound of her father's footsteps. He was coming through the hall. Harriet was too much agitated to encounter him. "She could not compose herself—Mr. Woodhouse would be alarmed—she had better go"—with most ready encouragement from her friend, therefore, she passed off through another door—and the moment she was gone, this was the spontaneous burst of Emma's feelings: "Oh

> God! that I had never seen her!"
>
> The rest of the day, the following night, were hardly enough for her thoughts.—She was bewildered amidst the confusion of all that had rushed on her within the last few hours. Every moment had brought a fresh surprise; and every surprise must be matter of humiliation to her.—How to understand it all! How to understand the deceptions she had been thus practising on herself, and living under!—The blunders, the blindness of her own head and heart!—she sat still, she walked about, she tried her own room, she tried the shrubbery—in every place, every posture, she perceived that she had acted most weakly; that she had been imposed on by others in a most mortifying degree; that she had been imposing on herself in a degree yet more mortifying; that she was wretched, and should probably find this day but the beginning of wretchedness.

The acute aesthetic pleasure of this turns on the counterpoint between Emma's spontaneous cry "Oh God! that I had never seen her!" and the exquisite comic touch of "she sat still, she walked about, she tried her own room, she tried the shrubbery—in every place, every posture, she perceived that she had acted most weakly." The acute humiliation of the will could not be better conveyed than by "she tried the shrubbery" and "every posture." Endlessly imaginative, Emma must now be compelled to endure the mortification of reducing herself to the postures and places of those driven into corners by the collapse of visions that have been exposed as delusions. Jane Austen, who seems to have identified herself with Emma, wisely chose to make this moment of ironic reversal a temporary purgatory, rather than an infernal discomfiture.

The Imagination of Emma Woodhouse

Stuart M. Tave

Emma Woodhouse is an "imaginist"; that is a nonce word, invented for her, according to the *OED*. There is that special charm in Emma, who always deserves the best treatment because she never puts up with any other, which demands a word of her own. A word made for her, and this very one, is surely the best treatment deserved by the Emma whose imagination creates a world of its own. It is a world made to a boundless perfection by desire, for in that dominion conferred by the imagination there are no limits upon life, either upon what can be known or what can be done. Emma's perfection is limited only by her imagination. But the truth is that her extraordinarily active imagination is surprisingly limited. It gives her none of that controlling power she is certain she wields over the finest details of life, not in action and not in understanding. That command of propriety and delicacy, her high value for elegance, and her mind at ease in its own world are the very things it takes from her. It is a humbling experience to discover that the real beauty of the world is not something to be made by the imagination but resides in the simple truth, and to find that the truth is so much more moving, so much more difficult to see, altogether a larger achievement of spirit. With Mr. Knightley we are happy she is capable of the mortification, because Emma is too good to be no better than perfect.

If Jane Austen had a special liking for Emma, one reason is that her own special subject, early and late, was the eighteenth-century problems

From *Some Words of Jane Austen*. ©1973 by The University of Chicago. University of Chicago Press, 1973.

and pleasures of imagination. It is not only in the juvenilia and the early novels, where we would expect familiar eighteenth-century materials, that we find girls of quick imagination and less judgment, Catharine Percival or Catherine Morland or Marianne Dashwood. Mr. Parker of *Sanditon*, we are told very soon, has "more Imagination than Judgement" and in meeting his sisters we see that we are in "a family of Imagination & quick feelings"; he finds his vent as a Projector and they in their fancy of suffering ill health. Sir Edward Denham of the same story has read more sentimental novels than agreed with him; his "fancy" has been caught by all the impassioned and most exceptionable parts and with "a perversity of Judgement," which must be attributed to his not having a very strong head, he is interested and inflamed to emulate the villains of the novels. How Jane Austen would have managed these varied imaginations, playing them against Charlotte Heywood and Sidney Parker and Clara Brereton, who see through them, would have been a major part of the development. In this respect, at least, *Sanditon* offers us quite familiar material and language, and in its use of terms like "Projector" (and "enthusiast") for the particular form of Mr. Parker's aberrant imagination its language has an early eighteenth-century sound. Readers of Swift as well as Johnson, and of a hundred lesser observers of possessed humanity, would have recognized its validity.

The contrasting of "imagination" or "fancy" or "wit" with "judgment" or "understanding" or "reason"—all the terms are used and all are important in *Emma*—is a commonplace in the writers of the eighteenth-century; it was in language philosophical, moral, and literary, and it was part of the language of common life. For our present purpose the multiple variations of the eighteenth-century history are of less importance than the broad oppositions. The judgment makes careful distinctions, usually working with patience and with study, separating facts from errors, discerning just relations and distinguishing proprieties. It is interested in determining truth. The imagination, less concerned with real differences, ranges widely and moves quickly, sees similarities or makes its own agreeable combinations and unities, guided by its feelings. It is interested in finding pleasure. Imagination has a larger part in poetry than in other pursuits; poetry is the art of uniting "pleasure" with "truth" by calling "imagination" to the help of "reason," Dr. Johnson said. The poet needs the proper balance: he needs the spirit and liveliness of imagination and he needs the judgment that controls what would otherwise be the unnatural and wandering tendencies of imagination, its disregard for the nature of things. The serious dangers of the unguarded imagination are in common life, where its extravagances can take possession not of a poem, not of a romance, but a mind. That was a problem Johnson knew, bitterly, in himself. He prayed and struggled against the strength of his own imagination, wicked, depraved, sinful, corrupt, and tyrannous over him. In his published work, in *Rasselas* especially, he writes as powerfully as any man ever has on that hunger of imagination which preys incessantly upon life, on the general human problem of "The Dangerous Prevalence of Imagination" (the title of chap. 44). Imagination is a formidable and obstinate disease of the intellect; when radicated by time its remedy is one of the hardest tasks of reason and virtue. It was a disease that he studied, especially in himself, with fearful cause. Madness is occasioned by too much indulgence of imagination. If Emma's story is nothing so somber as this, is a glorious comedy, it is her good fortune, because her story would not be quite so comic if Emma were not yet twenty-one and her fault of mind not yet a disease radicated by time. Nor would it move with such security to its happy remedy if she had not that clear-your-mind and rather Johnsonian figure of Mr. Knightley watching and correcting its course. Even so, and with the many other forces within and without her that ensure her safety, what her imagination leads her to is a most serious set of consequences for others and for herself.

The danger of a prevailing imagination, what makes it central for Johnson and Jane Austen, in their very different ways, is that imagination reshapes the world, and the self, to the desires of the mind. Imagination submits the shows of things to the desires of the mind, not as the poet but as the Quixote who loses the distinction between the real and the fanciful. Turning from the difficult work of seeing and understanding what is before it and within it, and the exertion of acting upon that knowledge, the mind bends the world to its own wants. It breaks bounds, emancipates itself from space and time, raises itself above the limiting human conditions, assumes higher powers, subjects things to its own will, makes all perfect. It makes its romance, sometimes of a pleasurable alarm, usually of pleasurable self-importance, whatever it craves. The desperation that had seized Marianne Dashwood at sixteen and a half, that she would never see a man who could "satisfy her ideas of perfection," had been rash and unjustifiable: "Willoughby was all that her fancy had delineated in that unhappy hour and in every brighter period." And when Colonel Brandon replaces him Brandon is embellished by Mrs. Dashwood's "active fancy, which fashioned every thing delightful to her, as it chose."

"That very dear part of Emma, her fancy," is dear to her because it gives her so much pleasure in making up her own truth. Harriet, who has no penetration, cannot tell who her parents are, so that "Emma was obliged to fancy what she liked"; but fancying what she likes is just the obligation Emma loves to assume. She has views of improving her little friend's mind but they come to nothing because it is easier to chat than to study, "much pleasanter to let her imagination range and work at Harriet's fortune, than to be labouring to enlarge her comprehension or exercise it on sober facts"; the only mental provision, appropriately, is the collection of riddles and the obfuscation of facts that follows. It was as Mr. Knightley had predicted: she will never submit to anything requiring industry and patience, "and a subjection of the fancy to the understanding." Facts become what the private light of the fancy wills, and when they are not there she invents them. Others are in the dark, she tells Harriet, removing Robert Martin by bringing forward the idea of Mr. Elton: "Hitherto I fancy you and I are the only people to whom his looks and manners have explained themselves." She then conjures up the entire scene of Mr. Elton and what he is doing at the moment with Harriet's picture and how he is showing it to his mother and sister and what he is saying to them and how they are responding. "How cheerful, how animated, how suspicious, how busy their imaginations all are!" Harriet smiles and her smiles grow stronger. A whole secret, and nonexistent, world has been created and conferred. The adventure of Harriet, Frank, and the gypsies presents a similar constructive opportunity to Emma, to "an imaginist, like herself," on fire with speculations and foresight, especially with such a groundwork of anticipation as her mind has already made. She sees the event as a very extraordinary thing, dependent on several coincidences, all making a unity in her mind—as if everything united to promise the most interesting consequences and making it impossible the occurrence should not bring Frank and Harriet together. But Emma as artist is defined by her position in this incident: with her old father and her little nephews, the only others to whom the story remains a significant pleasure. Mr. Woodhouse is comforted by his neighbors' inquiries after himself and his daughter and he has the pleasure of returning the answer that they are very indifferent; which is not exactly true, as Emma knows, because he must invent illnesses for her. The gypsies have in fact disappeared before the panic began and the whole history dwindles into unimportance, except for Emma and her nephews: "—in her imagination it maintained its ground," and they still ask every day for the story and tenaciously set her right if she varies in the slightest particular from the original recital.

We may not like Emma, and Jane Austen foresaw that possibility, but if she causes us discomfort it is because we cannot disown kinship with her. As Imlac says in establishing our kinship with the mad astronomer of *Rasselas*, there is no man whose imagination does not sometimes predominate over his reason, and under certain conditions it will begin to influence speech and action. Emma is rather like that lonely astronomer who thought he controlled the weather. The marriage of Miss Taylor leaves Emma in the great danger of suffering from intellectual solitude. Like the astronomer, having little to keep her busy or to divert her she finds pleasure in her own thoughts and conceives herself as what she is not, for who is pleased with what he is? Emma has a disposition to think a little too well of herself and, as Johnson says elsewhere, we always think ourselves better than we are and are generally desirous that others should think us still better than we think ourselves; that is what enables the flatterer to fill the imagination and make his appeal to human vanity (*Rambler* no. 104). Frank Churchill understands that. Emma's imagination amuses her desires and confers upon her a dominion, not over the heavens, but over the large and populous village of Highbury and the course of true love. She takes credit not for the sun and rain but for the match of Miss Taylor and Mr. Weston, though with no better reason. From there her mind begins to make up scene after scene, uniting and making combinations that delight, and her action begins.

The imagination is "lively" and gives added life; it gives power over life, over others and one's self, and Emma enjoys the power of having rather too much her own way. Rasselas admits, as Imlac finishes, that he too has his daydreams of ruling in perfection. Emma, like him, has some excuse for such ranging thoughts, having lived too long at the center of a happy little enclosure, seeming to unite in herself and her home some of the best blessings of existence. She has no equals in Highbury, where the Woodhouses are first in consequence and all look up to them. Mr. Woodhouse can command the visits of his own little circle, in great measure as he likes. In this circle there are the Westons, Mr. Knightley, and Mr. Elton, and after them there is a "second set," the Bateses and Mrs. Goddard, who introduces Harriet. Beyond this Emma has seen little, so that Harriet's talk of the Martins amuses her by such a picture of "another set of beings," such an "order of people" with whom she feels she can have nothing to do. Noting later the easy conceit of Mrs. Elton, Emma can fairly suppose that the lady has been "the best of her own set," which is a fair supposition, but there is a Mrs. Elton in every set. Mr. Woodhouse cannot suspect that Emma is not "thought perfect by every body," and, with one exception, which is not particularly agreeable to Emma, he is right. "Can you imagine any thing nearer perfect beauty than Emma altogether—face and figure?" Mrs. Weston asks. Beautiful she is, but Mrs. Weston is a fondly biased witness, concealing imperfection when she can in those for whom she is anxious. And if, among young men, "Mr. Elton is the standard of perfection in Highbury, both in person and mind" ("Very true," says Miss Bates), the standard is not high. Emma sees the standard well enough, but she is not prepared to give up her perfection among the women and she has less scruple and much less compunction toward what she calls, not pleasantly, the "amiable, upright, perfect Jane Fairfax." Jane Fairfax is not perfect; Mr. Knightley sees that without ascribing to her the very reprehensible feelings that Emma imagines. Even Mrs. Elton is prepared to see that Jane's character needs a supplement, and offers herself, very much in the spirit of imagination coming to the aid of judgment: "My liveliness and your solidity would produce perfection." But Emma will not share her perfection. She is clever, spoiled by being the cleverest of her family—like a fairy, her father says, and not so absurdly because she has in fact thrown a charm over the senses of her circle, thinks she knows what bewitches the senses of men and satisfies their judgment. With her quotation from *A Midsummer Night's Dream* she undertakes the fairy-like function of supervising the course of true love and doing the job rather more smoothly. Like Puck she stands above the fools; she plays tricks, she acts a part, she mimics. Above the mortal action, so charming as she is she sees no one who charms her, no one very superior who can tempt her to love and to a change of situation: "I cannot really change for the better." She is exempt from the ordinary way of human nature, falling in love, for "it is not my way, or my nature." That clever and delightfully superior Emma has the quickness and assurance of the imaginative mind, she has the "quick eye"—"Such an eye!" Mrs. Weston says, "and so brilliant!"—that makes her sufficiently acquainted with Robert Martin as soon as she sees him, that discerns the consciousness of Mr. Elton when she imagines the cause of his charade and his visit. She has that ability to see into others, the "instinctive knowledge" which is the gift of imagination. Nobody else could have had any idea that Frank Churchill was in love with Jane Fairfax, Harriet says, but Miss Woodhouse perhaps might, she "who can see into everybody's heart," she may have "imagined" it. But that last expression of faith is not fully gratifying at the moment it is delivered. "My dear Harriet," she says as Harriet is revealing the substantial confusion, "I perfectly remember the substance. . . ." "My dear Emma," Mr. Knightley had asked with earnest kindness, "do you think you perfectly understand the degree of acquaintance between the gentleman and lady . . . ?" "Oh! yes, perfectly. — Why do you make a doubt of it?"

One result is nonsense, and there is a lot of nonsense in Emma. It's part of the pleasure of knowing her, but then it's not all innocent either. It begins early and it has unpleasant results, in her first quarrel with Mr. Knightley, when he is indignant with Harriet's foolishness in refusing Robert Martin. Emma assumes she knows why the refusal is incomprehensible to Mr. Knightley: "A man always imagines a woman to be ready for anybody who asks her." But Mr. Knightley sweeps her off in his best Johnsonian way. "Nonsense! a man does not imagine any such thing" and as he goes on to discover what has happened it is clear that he means just what he says. In "common language," Thomas Reid said, "sense always implies judgment," so that a man of sense is a man of judgment and good sense is good judgment. "Nonsense is what is evidently contrary to right judgment. Common sense is that degree of judgment which is common to men with whom we can converse and transact business" ("Of Judgment," *Essays on the Intellectual Powers of Man*, Edinburgh, 1785). Faced with the results of a later miserable business Emma realizes that common sense would have directed her to converse differently with Harriet. "'But, with common sense,' she added, 'I am afraid I have had little to do.'" The nonsense of her imagination is an abuse of judgment in which she has not elevated her gifted mind but madly sunk it below the level necessary for common life. "Better be without sense," Mr. Knightley says, "than misapply it as you do." To him her defense of what she has done because of her estimates of the relative gentility of Harriet and Robert Martin is "Nonsense, errant nonsense, as ever was talked!" She is a decisive judge of the nonsense of others, of Mr. Elton or of Frank, but without recognition of her own responsibility for inducing it in the one and without understanding its intentions in the other. Frank is adroit and shameless in the use of nonsense to blind others, can make himself talk it very agreeably, and Emma is his readiest dupe. It is at Box Hill, where "Any nonsense will serve" that nonsense makes Emma lose her sense. And seeing her conduct, finally, with a clearness which had never blessed her before, she is ready to give it the name of "madness".

So Emma is the story of a girl of too much imagination. But there is another way of saying that.

The great Mrs. Churchill of *Emma*, whom we never see but who is so disagreeable that she can clear her ill-fame only by dying, is in one point fully justified in death. No one had ever believed her to be seriously ill. "The event acquitted her of all the fancifulness, and all the selfishness of imaginary complaints." As a matter of fact, she doesn't deserve even that small justice, because she had been carried off after a short struggle by a sudden seizure of a different nature from anything foreboded by her general state. There is a deficiency of imagination in almost every character in the book, even Mrs. Churchill, even those who acquit her and attribute to her a suffering "more than any body had ever supposed" and to Mr. Churchill such a dreadful loss that he would never get over it. That deficiency is pervasive because the nature of characters of various sorts is such that they cannot imagine certain kinds of possibilities. Mrs. Churchill was known to be a capricious woman when Mr. Weston had given up his son to her, "but it was not in Mr. Weston's nature to imagine" that any caprice could affect one so dear to him as Frank. When Mrs. John Knightley heard of Miss Taylor's marriage she so grieved for Mr. Woodhouse and Emma, because, as she says, "I could not imagine how you could possibly do without her." Miss Bates always makes a point of reading to herself Jane's letters before reading them aloud to Mrs. Bates, for fear of there being anything in them that will be distressing, but when she read that Jane was unwell she burst out quite frightened with an exclamation. "I cannot imagine," she says later, "how I could be so off my guard!" If, near the conclusion of the novel, poor Mr. Woodhouse could know the marriage that Mr. Knightley is plotting in his heart he would care less for the state of Mr. Knightley's lungs; "but without the most distant imagination" of the impending evil, without the slightest perception, totally unsuspicious, he is quite comfortable. He has a "favouring blindness," as it is called on an earlier and similar occasion. Mr. Knightley, under the happy influence of his successful love, not yet publicly known, forgets an appointment with Mr. Elton; the important Mrs. Elton, whose world is very small, feels the indignity done her husband: "I cannot imagine . . . I cannot imagine how he could do such a thing by you, of all people in the world!" Reality comes to each of these characters through such a selective vision, shaped by their own capacities and needs, that much of it is simply excluded.

But what seems to be true is that a deficiency of imagination is the necessary correlate of an excess of imagination within a narrow range of concern. Mrs. John Knightley cannot imagine how an ordinary event can be possible, but when there is a report of snow at Christmas (half an inch, it turns out) she is all alarm: "The horror of being blocked up at Randalls, while her children were at Hartfield, was full in her imagination." Miss Bates may not be able to imagine herself off guard (though the reader never sees her in any other condition), but she is so, in this instance, because she "fancied" a bad illness for Jane. Mr. Woodhouse cannot imagine Mr. Knightley marrying Emma because his mind is fully occupied with an imaginary anxiety that Mr. Knightley may have taken cold. Mrs. Elton cannot imagine how Mr. Knightley could have any unknown engagement more important than a meeting with her husband, but a few moments earlier she has been delighting herself in an anxious parade of mystery about Jane's engagement, "fancying herself" acquainted with secret knowledge of forthcoming marriages. Nor is it merely the silly, or even less intelligent, whose imagination cannot function under certain circumstances. Mrs. Weston, as an example, knows her sanguine husband is always expecting Frank to make his first appearance while she, sensibly, is more restrained; but it means more to her than it does to her husband that Frank should pay his visit: "I cannot bear to imagine any reluctance on his side." It is the remark of a sensitive woman and we must like and respect her for it—Mr. Knightley appreciates what is going on in her mind—but Mrs. Weston is trying to avoid seeing a truth, as she does elsewhere when affection leads her.

To say, then, of Emma that she has too much imagination is to say that she has too little imagination. There are certain things she cannot imagine. John Knightley gives her a sly and sharp hint that Mr. Elton is interested in her. She is astonished: "are you imagining me to be Mr. Elton's object?" "Such an imagination has crossed me, I own Emma; and if it never occurred to you before, you may as well take it into consideration now." It is not an idea Emma can entertain seriously and she is amused at the blunders that arise from partial knowledge and the mistakes which people of "high pretensions to judgment" are forever falling into; nor is she pleased with Mr. John Knightley "for imagining her blind and ignorant." As Mr. Elton on the fateful evening moves physically closer to her, Emma cannot avoid the internal suggestion of "Can it really be as my brother imagined?" Similarly, just after Emma has, by "the judicious law of her own brain" determined how she will promote the match of Harriet and Frank Churchill, Mr. Knightley begins to suspect some relationship between Frank and Jane Fairfax. "I have lately imagined," he says to Emma, "that I saw symptoms of attachment between them." She is excessively amused: "I am delighted to find that you can vouchsafe to let your imagination wander—but it will not do—very sorry to check you in your first essay—but indeed it will not do." But it is of course Emma's imagination that will not do what needs doing. The Emma who sees into everybody's heart never "imagined," "never had the slightest suspicion," of Frank Churchill's having the least regard for Jane Fairfax.

The imagination offers a freedom to the mind, a freely ranging and lively activity, the quick eye that is not held by a limited vision, the insight into what is otherwise hidden. But the paradox of imagination, as Johnson had understood, is that it fixes its attention upon one train of ideas and gains its gratification by rejecting and excluding what it does not want. Seeing more, in its own conceit, it sees less, and having put its own shape upon the world it cannot conceive what lies beyond its preconceptions. Emma closes herself off from seeing or hearing. The same symptoms in Mr. Elton that lead John Knightley to imagine what his object may be are lost on her, "too eager and busy in her own previous conceptions and views to hear him impartially, or see him with clear vision." While she is fancying what she likes for Harriet her infatuation for that girl blinds her, as the imagination becomes the victim of its own creation. She takes charge of the mind of lesser fancy, "could not feel a doubt of having given Harriet's fancy a proper direction" toward Mr. Elton. Harriet accepts that direction because whatever Miss Woodhouse says is always right—"but otherwise I could not have imagined it." Emma is reassuring: "Receive it on my judgment." Those words return upon her in the later astonishment that Harriet could have the presumption to raise her thoughts to Mr. Knightley: "How could she dare to fancy herself the chosen of such a man . . . !" But if the inferiority of mind or situation is little felt, who but herself had taught Harriet? While Emma has been teaching Harriet how to elevate her imagination, Harriet has been giving Emma's imagination not more opportunity but less. Harriet has been the very worst sort of companion Emma could have, fulfilling Mr. Knightley's prediction. "How can Emma imagine she has any thing to learn herself, while Harriet is presenting such a delightful inferiority?"

By limiting reality to its own ideas the imagination loses its control not only of others but of itself and is then controlled by what possesses it. Taking up an idea and "running away" with it is a common failing, one that Mrs. Elton warns Mr. Weston against, though that is obviously advice she herself needs rather more; it is a fault that Miss Bates recognizes in herself, which gives her some self-knowledge Emma lacks. Emma may find Miss Bates ridiculous in her uncontrolled talk, but Emma is very like her: Miss Bates knows that now and then "I have let a thing escape me which I should not"; Emma knows she should not have betrayed her suspicion of Jane's feelings to Frank Churchill, because it is hardly right, "but it had been so strong an idea, that it would escape her." Frank is so complimentary to her penetration that she isn't certain she ought to have held her tongue. As with Miss Bates there is much running away in a mind that is subject to its own desires. Emma can be acute in argument, as she is when warning Mrs. Weston about running away with the idea that Mr. Knightley may be attached to Jane ("proof only shall convince me"), but it is an argument in which sound thought serves her emotion and it reveals how little knowledge she has of her own mind and heart. For all its power and all its desires Emma's imagination is weakest in understanding her own desires. She can describe so well what a man ought to be and how "She could fancy such a man," without any recognition that she has seen and heard such a man all her life.

The Closure of *Emma*

John Hagan

In spite of the large body of rich and sensitive criticism on *Emma*, two major aspects of the novel have received relatively little attention: the way in which Emma's behavior in several chapters following the proposal scene in volume 3, chapter 13, throws essential light on the nature and extent of her reformation, and the way in which Mr. Knightley's behavior in the same chapters and in the proposal scene itself throws essential light on his character and function. One important reason for the comparative neglect of these matters, I suspect, is the reader's realization that the hero's proposal to the heroine in a Jane Austen novel is a foregone conclusion, and his expectation (not entirely unfounded) that the events which follow it will be a routine and more or less anticlimactic tying-together of the loose odds and ends of the plot. His attention relaxes, and he tends to skim over this material because he anticipates no surprises. However this may be, ignoring the closure of *Emma* has often resulted in an underestimation of a number of the subtleties in Jane Austen's characterization of the novel's two central figures and the extreme care she has taken to conform to the standards of fictional realism—psychological, moral, and circumstantial alike.

A crucial example of such underestimation is the view, held by a great many critics, that the decisive changes which take place in Emma's character during the action and come to a climax in the insight which she achieves in the famous self-recognition scene of volume 3, chapter 11,

From *Studies in English Literature 1500–1900* 15, no. 4 (Autumn 1975).

constitute an unqualified reformation. Edgar F. Shannon, Jr., for example, speaks of Emma's "complete redemption," her attainment of "full awareness," and throughout his article uses highly honorific terms and phrases, like "regeneration," "transformation," and "progress from self-deception and vanity to perception and humility," which have obvious religious connotations and suggest a process completed to the entire satisfaction of both author and reader. Even when critics do not explicitly assert that the changes Emma has gone through are "complete" or "full," some, like Wayne C. Booth, W. A. Craik, and Joseph Wiesenfarth seem to imply this by the fact that their remarks about Emma's correcting her faults, achieving "genuine reform," attaining "moral and emotional maturity," and being "profoundly changed in the course of the story," are made without any reservations. Similarly, it has been almost universally assumed that Mr. Knightley's chief function in the novel is to serve as the moral norm, the *raisonneur*, the more or less infallible embodiment of those very qualities of reason, good sense, moderation, prudence, clarity of vision, and so forth, which Emma so conspicuously lacks at the beginning, but to the full attainment of which the main action of the novel eventually takes her. Arnold Kettle's claim that Mr. Knightley's "judgment is recommended [by the novel] as invariably sound" has been echoed by many.

Of course, none of these interpretations has gone unchallenged. Marvin Mudrick, Joseph M. Duffy, Jr., Mark Schorer, Howard S. Babb, and A. Walton Litz have called the completeness of Emma's reformation into serious question, while Duffy, Craik, and various others—Andrew H. Wright, Frank W. Bradbrook, W. J. Harvey, and Yasmine Gooneratne—have also impugned the authority of Mr. Knightley. Indeed, the main weakness of the interpretations these critics reject is apparent: they make *Emma* sound too much like an allegory of redemption. For, however much the bildungsroman—the genre to which *Emma* obviously belongs—may ultimately be indebted to such allegories, to ancient myths of pilgrimage, purification, and salvation, to traditional "spiritual autobiographies," and the like, Jane Austen's novel is also securely rooted in a convention of fictional realism which precludes precisely the sort of moral and psychological simplifications these rejected readings ascribe to it. Dickens, with his strong penchant toward allegory, fable, and fairy-tale, may find moral paragons and total conversions a necessity for his art, but Jane Austen does not.

Nevertheless, so difficult is it to do justice to all the fine shades of tone and meaning in *Emma* that the critics I have just named fall into difficulties of their own. Mudrick, Duffy, and Schorer actually wonder whether Emma has changed very much for the better, after all. Clearly, this is going too far. But it is just as easy not to go far enough. Babb and Litz concede that Emma does remain flawed to the end, but structure their arguments and rhetoric so that the flaws they indicate do not receive much emphasis and seem to have little significance in the novel's total design.

As for those critics who question the reliability of Mr. Knightley himself, here too there has been a tendency to stop short of a full statement of the case. A charge sometimes brought against Mr. Knightley is the way in which his jealousy arouses his prejudice against Frank Churchill. But beyond simply noting this most of the commentators offer little or no discussion of it. Indeed, the importance of this limitation in Mr. Knightley is sometimes drastically minimized. In spite of his jealousy of Frank, Wright asserts, Mr. Knightley's "basic common sense" is never vitiated. Even in the chapter where his quarrel with Emma about the meaning of Frank's delayed arrival first makes his jealousy glaringly apparent, and where Emma herself quite correctly observes, "'We are both prejudiced; you against, I for him,'" Wright sees Knightley as performing only "his usual role of *raisonneur*." Craik, Wiesenfarth, and Gooneratne, too, rush to the defense with the argument that "his jealousy is not unreasonable and . . . his dislike is justified"—overlooking the fact that by the end of volume 1 Mr. Knightley has formed a highly unfavorable opinion of Frank's character even before the latter has appeared on the scene, and that to whatever extent Frank's subsequent conduct may verify that opinion, it is based originally on very insufficient evidence. Surely, it is no merit in Mr. Knightley that if he happens to reach a right conclusion, it is for quite the wrong reasons.

It is clear, then, that certain basic problems of the nature and extent of Emma's reformation and of the character and function of Mr. Knightley have not been dealt with by recent critics in an entirely satisfactory way. There is, however, one outstanding exception to this disappointing pattern of commentary: J. F. Burrows's *Jane Austen's Emma*, which is perhaps the finest—certainly the longest and more minutely detailed—study of *Emma* yet published. Burrows's keen ear for Jane Austen's subtlest nuances and his ability to see the text freshly have enabled him to achieve a major breakthrough in interpretation. As he clearly demonstrates, the choice offered us by the commentators between an Emma who does not basically change and an Emma who changes completely is absurdly false. Just as in real life "self-knowledge is not an absolute state to which a person attains in a single moment of insight," but "is an erratic progress from one solution to a fresh problem, punctuated at best by moments of insight but too often marked by lapses and regressions, a stumbling progress ending only when life ends," so in the novel "Emma is actually shown as coming only to a better, not a perfect, knowledge of herself and the meaning of her actions." Similarly, Burrows scotches the simplistic view of Mr. Knightley's infallible authority. For the first time the way in which the latter's jealousy distorts his views is not only analyzed in detail, but is given the major emphasis its prominent role in the text requires. And from this, as well as other facts, the conclusion that he "cannot be regarded as the author's spokesman and chief guardian of her values," because he is only "one fallible creature among others," necessarily follows.

Yet, full though Burrows's demonstrations of these propositions are, what he himself calls the "inexhaustible richness" of *Emma* will always be an invitation to further discussion. What follows, therefore, is an attempt to lend additional support to his interpretations by an examination of some new evidence, which will be drawn specifically, as I announced at the beginning of this article, from the proposal scene and several chapters (14–16, 18–19) which follow it. Burrows's treatment of the former overlooks one of the most important questions it raises, namely, Mr. Knightley's reason for proposing at all, and his discussion of the subsequent scenes ignores some of the major implications of Mr. Knightley's change of attitude toward Harriet, of Emma's silence to Mr. Knightley about her second matchmaking scheme, of her plot to send Harriet off to London, and of her reaction to her discovery of Harriet's true parentage.

II

At the beginning of the proposal scene, we remember, Emma is laboring under the illusion that Mr. Knightley has fallen in love with Harriet and "might be watching for encouragement" to confess this fact. Naturally, given her own love for him, she resolves to deny him this encouragement—until, seeing the pain which her enforcement of silence causes him, she retracts her decision and magnanimously urges him to speak. This places her in a position where, it appears, it might be necessary for her to reveal that Harriet returns his love. But just at this critical juncture Mr. Knightley proposes to Emma herself, and she is able "to rejoice that Harriet's secret had not escaped her, and to resolve that it need not and should not." Mr. Knightley's later praise of "'the beauty of truth and sincerity'" in human dealings elicits from her only "a blush of sensibility on Harriet's account, which she could not give any sincere explanation of"; and still later, when he attributes to her tutelage whatever good qualities Harriet may possess, she shakes her head in denial, checks herself in the midst of exclaiming, "'Ah! poor Harriet!'" and submits "quietly to a little more praise than she deserved." The "necessity of concealment from Mr. Knightley" and "the disguise, equivocation, mystery, so hateful to her to practise" will be brought to an end, she resolves, only after she and Mr. Knightley have married, for only then will she be willing to give him "that full and perfect confidence which her disposition was most ready to welcome as a duty."

Now it is certainly tempting to interpret this silence on Emma's part simply as generosity and compassion. By falling in love with Mr. Knightley, Harriet has acted foolishly, and therefore in what better way can Emma show kindness toward the girl than by at least concealing her folly from Mr. Knightley himself, especially since Emma has in some measure been responsible for her infatuation by unwittingly encouraging it? But such an explanation oversimplifies. Emma's own appearance in Mr. Knightley's eyes is as much at stake as Harriet's, and therefore her having played a part in encouraging Harriet's infatuation establishes not only the duty of silence for Harriet's sake, but the prudence of silence for herself. If concern for saving Harriet's face is an element in Emma's motivation—as it surely is—so too is a concern for saving her own.

This is suggested partly by her thinking of her silence as a "service," for that word and several others used more or less synonymously ("kind undertaking," "kind designs," "use," "usefulness," "friendly arrangement," "friendship") appeared frequently in the early chapters of the novel as an ironical commentary on the way in which Emma rationalized away the considerable element of self-interest and vanity in her seemingly benevolent concern for Harriet and her matchmaking scheme for the latter and Mr. Elton. Whenever Emma decides to perform a "service" for Harriet, these chapters forewarn us, we ought not to be too ready to accept Emma's interpretation of her motives as the only reliable one. In fact, that "blush of sensibility" with which she greets Mr. Knightley's praise of truth and sincerity gives her completely away. Were the purpose of her silence solely to perform the legitimate "service" of saving her friend from disgrace, it is hard to understand why she should react quite so self-consciously. Moreover, while her way of responding to Mr. Knightley's praise of Harriet and of the good he thinks she (Emma) has done her does indeed protect Harriet's reputation by concealing the fact of her foolish infatuation, it is clear that Emma's immediate intent in checking her head-shake of denial, in exclaiming,

"'Ah! poor Harriet!'" and in quietly submitting "to a little more praise than she deserved" is also to conceal from Mr. Knightley the fact that in encouraging that infatuation she did the girl more harm than good. Harriet is a "poor Harriet" not only because she has been more foolish than Mr. Knightley knows, but also because she has been Emma's victim. Again, if Emma's silence is motivated solely by an altruistic concern for Harriet's welfare, it is hard to see why she should regard it as "hateful"—a very strong word—or why she should dignify by the term "duty" only the confidence she intends giving to Mr. Knightley after their marriage, as if loyalty to a friend—especially to a friend one has injured—were not a solemn "duty" too. Indeed, on the assumption that Emma's motive has been simply to protect Harriet's reputation, her decision to reveal everything to Mr. Knightley after their marriage is unintelligible: whether he is told now or later, Harriet's image in his mind will still be tarnished. But if Emma's silence has also been prompted in large part by a desire to save her own face, then her decision makes perfect sense, for after she has secured Mr. Knightley this need not be as decisive a consideration as it was before. Presumably she will then be able to confess her sins with considerable assurance of ready absolution. Perhaps we are even to wonder whether Emma will confess at all! Is it not possibly a sly stroke of irony that Jane Austen speaks of nothing more than Emma's intentions, and never actually tells us whether she carries them out?

In any event, irony certainly does inhere in Emma's maneuver, immediately after the proposal scene, of sending Harriet off to spend a few weeks in London with Isabella. Shannon sees this plan as totally innocent; it "originates in charity." The inference would seem to be that it is thus a further sign of Emma's reformation. In sharp contrast, Mudrick sees Emma's purpose as nothing more than cynical self-interest: "she limits her compunction" and her relationship with Harriet to letters because she is unable to endure the embarrassment of meeting her victim face-to-face. But each of these interpretations is partial. Jane Austen's language is ingeniously contrived to invite both views, and thereby to reveal that Emma's motivation is complex, mixed, ambivalent. On the one hand, several passages make perfectly clear that Emma's sympathy for the embarrassment and disappointment Harriet experiences after learning that Emma and Mr. Knightley have become engaged is completely sincere; having twice led the naive girl astray in her romantic expectations, Emma is now extremely sensitive to her suffering. "How to do her best by Harriet . . . how to spare her from an unnecessary pain; how to make her any possible atonement; how to appear least her enemy" become her paramount concerns. "On these subjects, her perplexity and distress were very great — and her mind had to pass again and again through every bitter reproach and sorrowful regret that had ever surrounded it." "When remembering how disappointed a heart was near her, how much might at that moment . . . be enduring by the feelings which she had led astray herself," she is "haunted" by a "sense of injustice, of guilt, of something most painful." Thus, the plan of hurrying Harriet off to London recommends itself to Emma's compassion as a way of giving the girl some relief. On the other hand — and by the same token — it affords Emma herself relief — relief from the pain caused her by contemplating Harriet's pain and also from the pain of experiencing a face-to-face encounter with Harriet's resentment. By describing Emma's plan as "one scheme more," and thereby relating it to the matchmaking schemes, in which self-interest played a conspicuous part, Jane Austen clearly seems to be implying this motive, even if we assume that Emma herself is using this phrase in her thoughts with some measure of self-irony. Certainly, the relief Emma clearly does feel at Harriet's departure both in anticipation and after the fact seems too great for it to be attributable to altruistic feeling alone. The language on this point is especially emphatic:

> To have Harriet removed from the scene would be "inexpressibly desirable."
>
> Once the letter to her has been written, it takes only "half an hour" of Mr. Knightley's company to reinstate Emma "in a proper share of the happiness of the evening before," when he proposed to her.
>
> Though the prospect of Harriet's necessary exclusion from Hartfield after the marriage causes Emma to regret the girl's "unmerited punishment," she "could not deplore her future absence as any deduction from her own enjoyment," for with her burden of resentment "Harriet would be rather a dead weight than otherwise."
>
> It was a very great relief to Emma to find Harriet as desirous as herself to avoid a meeting. Their intercourse was painful enough by letter. How much worse had they been obliged to meet!"
>
> And once Harriet has gone, the "true happiness" Emma so speedily finds in Mr. Knightley's company prompts the author's wry observation that "the difference of Harriet at Mrs. Goddard's, or in London, made perhaps an unreasonable difference in Emma's sensations."

That Emma's hope in sending Harriet off to London even extends beyond merely escaping the girl's resentment into softening it is suggested by her expectation that Harriet will see her action as "a proof of attention and kindness in herself, from whom every thing was due." The irony in all these passages is that altruism and self-interest are intimately blended. Though Emma has been greatly changed by her experiences in the course of the novel, something of her old self still remains.

This old self is also evidenced by traces, appearing up to the very end of the novel, of Emma's snobbery. Some critics have insisted, of course, that as a result of her development this snobbery is completely purged. In a broad, general sense, obviously, this is undeniable, as Emma's eventual perception of true gentility in Robert Martin and her contrite resolution to begin "a regular, equal, kindly intercourse" with Miss Bates prove. But such an interpretation coarsens the fine texture of Jane Austen's characterization by overlooking the crucial evidence of the passage in the concluding chapter (beginning "Harriet's parentage became known" which describes Emma's reaction to her discovery of Harriet's true birth. Apart from Mudrick, who clearly sees Emma's snobbery here, even critics who do take note of this passage seem to be embarrassed by it. Shannon, trying to rebut Mudrick, asserts that far from being guilty of "a supercilious aspersion upon Harriet," Emma is simply perceiving the truth—"that neither a Mr. Knightley, a Frank Churchill, nor a Mr. Elton (of any century) would, as she had fondly supposed, be inclined to marry an illegitimate girl of simple mind and unpropitious heritage." But Emma says nothing in this passage about Harriet's "simple mind"; she rests her objection to a match between Harriet and Mr. Knightley solely on the ground of her "unpropitious heritage." Earlier, it is true, upon first learning of Harriet's infatuation with Mr. Knightley, Emma did object to Harriet's "very inferior powers," but that was before she discovered the truth about Harriet's birth. Now, as the author's heavily satirical "unbleached" makes clear, it is only because she has since discovered that truth that even the major fact of Harriet's illegitimacy has become important to her. Babb runs into the same error when he too tries to take the sting out of the passage by arguing that "the status which Emma now assigns Harriet—no longer fancying her friend the daughter of some rich gentleman—is the same status which Mr. Knightley has assigned Harriet from the beginning." Mr. Knightley, however, objected to Emma's encouraging Harriet to look above the rank of Robert Martin not merely because of the girl's birth, but on the complex ground of her "'situation,'" "'nature,'" and "'education'" as well. Emma's objection reduces the issue to the single question of "nobility or wealth," and this is precisely wherein the comic irony and her snobbery lie.

The point in all these matters—Emma's snobbish reaction to her discovery of Harriet's true parentage, her plan of sending Harriet to London, and her silence to Mr. Knightley about her second match-making scheme—is not, needless to say, to suggest that Jane Austen's irony is any way crude or cynical, designed to debunk Emma or minimize the significance of her development. Quite the contrary, Emma does become a much more admirable person in the course of the action than she was at the beginning, and the central purpose of the novel is to show this. So much is unquestionable, and cannot be overemphasized. At the same time, however, her development occurs in such a way as never to violate (as a less accomplished artist might so easily have violated) the canons of realism within which Jane Austen has chosen to write. For if, as Booth has pointed out, it is crucial to Jane Austen's design that, in spite of Emma's faults, "she must remain sympathetic or the reader will not wish for and delight sufficiently in her reform," so it is also crucial that for all of the reformation she undergoes Emma remain believable, credible, human—in a word, fallible. She must never be transformed into a stick-figure of virtue, a paragon, a mere vehicle for didacticism. The love Booth says we feel for her even before her reformation would be irreparably compromised if, after her reformation, she were to emerge as a mere prig. It is all a matter of the most delicate nuances: her character must decisively improve, but the change must not be total, unshaded, or unqualified. The significance of the passages I have examined, with their emphasis upon the vestiges of snobbery in Emma's attitudes and the ambiguities of her motives, is that they are essential and brilliantly devised elements in the achievement of precisely this purpose.

III

The problem of adhering to her canons of realism, of avoiding allegory and fable, of refraining from transforming a character into a moral exemplum, also faces Jane Austen in her treatment of Mr. Knightley. Indeed, given the fact that one of the main roles he has to play throughout the book is that of Emma's mentor, the problem is even more acute with him than with her—especially since the posture in which we see him from the very first chapter to almost the end of volume 1 is that of a model of good sense, rationality, and prudence. If ever the odds were loaded in favor of a character's emerging as nothing more than a prig, they certainly are in Mr. Knightley's case. That he does not emerge as such, however, the critics seem unanimously to agree, and this is partly the result, as Burrows has shown, of the fact that from the last chapter of volume 1 to the proposal scene itself Mr. Knightley, far from remaining the man of poised and impeccable judgment he was at the beginning, falls under the sway of a powerful jealousy of Frank Churchill, whom he sees as a potential rival for Emma's love, and thus comes to react against him with the strongest prejudice. The measure of the intensity of this jealousy and prejudice is the way in which he makes a comically "instantaneous reappraisal" of Frank's character the moment he learns that Emma's love for that young man has never been real. As earlier he had been too harshly prejudiced *against* Frank, he now swings to the other extreme and becomes too strongly prejudiced *in his favor*. Only later, after reading Frank's letter of explanation, which shows him to be neither hero nor villain, but only a flawed yet attractive young man, who has achieved some recognition of his faults and seems to have a potential for still further improvement, does Mr. Knightley's view of him strike a fair balance. But, vital though all this is, it is not the only means by which Jane Austen demonstrates Mr. Knightley's engagingly human fallibility.

To appreciate fully the ironical significance of his jealousy, prejudice, and recantation *vis-à-vis* Frank, we also have to see how closely parallel they are to the pattern of Emma's earlier feelings toward Jane Fairfax in volume 2, chapters 8–16. Just as the prospect of Frank turning out to be his rival for Emma's love arouses Mr. Knightley's jealousy and hostility, so, earlier, Mrs. Weston's suggestion that Mr. Knightley might be falling in love with Jane Fairfax aroused Emma's jealousy and augmented the hostility she had been feeling toward Jane from the beginning. And just as Mr. Knightley's jealousy and hostility evaporate as soon as he learns the true nature of Emma's feelings for Frank, so Emma began to feel "more conscience-stricken about Jane Fairfax than she had often been"—in fact, adopted her first major resolutions to become more friendly with that girl—the moment Mr. Knightley vigorously dismissed Mrs. Weston's suggestion as nonsense. The only significant difference between the two situations is that whereas Mr. Knightley has been fully aware all along of his love for Emma, she had been in love with him only unconsciously. With ludicrous ignorance of her true feelings, she rationalized the distress caused her by Mrs. Weston's suggestion as a concern for the welfare of "little Henry," Mr. Knightley's nephew, who, if his uncle were to marry, might be cut out from Donwell, and she explained her changed attitude toward Jane simply as a response to Mr. Knightley's charge of neglect. But these differences, while contributing to the comedy, are less important than the parallels. For it is the latter which drive home the irony that there is a much greater kinship in fallibility between Mr. Knightley and Emma than our initial impression of them as wise mentor and foolish pupil would suggest.

Furthermore, there is an even greater irony at Mr. Knightley's expense in that, for all of her initial ignorance, it is the pupil who, in the long run, acquires fuller self-knowledge than the mentor. After discovering her love for Mr. Knightley, Emma also comes to see clearly that the reason she was duped for a time into imagining herself in love with Frank was simply that he flattered her vanity, and she is able to give herself "a saucy conscious smile" of understanding about the real nature of the feelings underlying her earlier concern for "little Henry." But there is no indication in the text that any comparable recognition is ever achieved by Mr. Knightley. Although he has long known about the existence of his jealousy itself, the way in which that jealousy has created his prejudice against Frank, and even the extent of that prejudice itself, seem to escape him. The abrupt modification of his attitude toward Frank which follows Emma's admission that she allowed the latter's attentions only because he flattered her vanity is rendered entirely in Mr. Knightley's spoken words. If Mr. Knightley has any awareness of the motives causing this about-face in his attitude, now would be the perfect time for Jane Austen to disclose it, but no such disclosure is forthcoming. So too, at the very end of the same chapter, the sly little comment on his changed opinion is not Mr. Knightley's own, but only the author's. When Jane Austen does reveal to us Mr. Knightley's thoughts in this chapter—and here is the last substantial revelation of them which the novel gives us—they are shown to be concerned solely with his feelings for Emma herself: the transition from magnanimous concern to hope which immediately precedes and prompts his proposal to her, and the happiness which follows her acceptance of it. The reader sees the causal connection between this development and the change in Mr. Knightley's attitude toward Frank, but there is not the slightest suggestion that Mr. Knightley himself does. Saucy, conscious smiles of self-recognition like Emma's are not for him.

Mr. Knightley also seems to be ignorant of the ironic implications of his comparable change of attitude toward Harriet. At the beginning of the novel, we recall, he can say nothing whatsoever in her favor. Apart from the disadvantages of her birth and her situation, she is no more in his eyes than a silly and ignorant little girl whose naive admiration of

Emma can only harm them both. Early in volume 3, however, Mr. Knightley suddenly begins to replace these harsh judgments with sentiments which are much more charitable; later, during the outing at Donwell, he and Harriet even walk together *tête-à-tête*; and by the end of the novel, he has come completely around to granting that Emma's original estimate of her protegée's good qualities was perfectly correct. At first glance, of course, the parallel between this reversal of attitude toward Harriet and the one toward Frank which took place earlier seems to be only superficial, for here Mr. Knightley does seem to understand the reason for his change: through frequent conversations with her, he has come to know Harriet much better; his prejudice against her, he now recognizes, was based simply on his ignorance; all he lacked was enough information. It must be insisted, however, that this explanation for Mr. Knightley's change of feeling toward Harriet is insufficient. Just as he fails to see how the disappearance of his jealousy contributed directly to the disappearance of his extreme hostility to Frank, so he now exaggerates the role played by impartial "observations" in the softening of his opinion of Harriet. His blindness in the former case is complicated by self-deception in the latter; he is falling into the same error Emma herself committed when she explained her changed attitude toward Jane simply as a response to Mr. Knightley's charge of neglect. For at the root of their motives is something deeper and more personal. What this is in Mr. Knightley's case is made clear by the fact that the beginning of his change of attitude toward Harriet coincides exactly in time with the beginning of her infatuation with him. The latter is precipitated by his "rescue" of her from Mr. Elton's snub at the Crown Inn ball, and it is just after this that he voices his opinion to Emma that "'Harriet Smith has some first-rate qualities,'" and is "'more conversable'" than he expected. Though Jane Austen does not explicitly point to a causal connection between these events, it does not seem likely in so meticulous and subtle an author that this sequence is the result of mere chance. Harriet's feelings on the occasion of the dance are very intense and quite visible. Needless to say, Mr. Knightley does not fully grasp the meaning of these signs; there is never any suggestion in the novel that he has the least suspicion that Harriet has fallen in love with him, and Emma keeps the fact a closely guarded secret. But to assume that he perceives Harriet's great and obvious pleasure in his company, that he himself is pleased by her response, and that, accordingly, he begins to modify his attitude toward her would seem completely justified. The point is not that fuller acquaintance with Harriet fails to contribute in some measure to this modification, but that the incentive to cultivate her acquaintance in the first place comes into existence only after her flattering behavior has created a predisposition in her favor, and that this predisposition, in turn, colors his subsequent observations themselves. It is one more ironic point of similarity between the master and the pupil, who had been earlier predisposed in Frank's favor because his attentions had flattered her vanity too—with the major difference, however, that the pupil comes to a full understanding of her motivation, whereas the master does not. It is Emma herself who tells us that her vanity was flattered; Mr. Knightley, lacking such self-knowledge, forces us back upon inference.

Such engaging fallibility, then, as we see in the motives for his shifting opinions of Frank and Harriet and his blindness to these motives is a key factor in preventing Mr. Knightley from becoming the stick-figure of virtue, the priggish paragon, which his role as Emma's mentor is always threatening to make him. But Mr. Knightley's humanity is also decisively revealed in an even subtler way when we consider the motive of his proposal of marriage to Emma. What prompts him to propose to her at the moment he does (vol. 3, chap. 13)? Why does he make his decision at precisely this point and no other?

With the exception of Wiesenfarth, critics in general have not given an explicit reply to these questions. But Wiesenfarth's answer would seem to be representative of what the other discussions commonly imply—namely, that

> Mr. Knightley . . . marries Emma, not because she is the mistress of Hartfield and first lady of Highbury, but *because she is finally a lovable person*. . . . The marriage of Emma to Mr. Knightley is the novel's culminating symbolic event. It can come only after Emma has put aside pretensions to superiority that are non-personal and after she has accepted reality as a condition for meaningful life. . . . Gradually Emma comes to see things as Mr. Knightley does. . . . Only then is she ready to be his wife. . . . Mr. Knightley was shaping her to be the woman who would be the perfect match for himself. . . . Emma's status as bride . . . is the outward confirmation of an inner change. . . . Once Emma knows herself and others, she is ready to accept the responsibility of the bride of George Knightley. (my italics)

Obviously, not all of these statements say exactly the same thing: some seem to refer more to Emma's motives than to Mr. Knightley's. But the impression they add up to is unmistakable: Mr. Knightley has refrained from proposing marriage to Emma before the scene in volume 3, chapter 13, because heretofore he has not found her worthy of him; she has not come up to his moral and intellectual standards. Once she has developed and reformed, however, and he has become aware of her maturation, he is ready and willing to accept her as his wife. His decision is a thoroughly rational and deliberate one arrived at after a calm scrutiny and assessment of the evidence.

But such an interpretation of Mr. Knightley's motives is demonstrably false. Quite apart from the fact that it posits an insufferable degree of priggishness which apparently no one has ever felt him to possess, and which, even more importantly, is incongruous with what we have seen is Jane Austen's ironic conception of his fallibility in other areas, it is an interpretation which is inconsistent with the simplest facts of the plot. Because we, as readers, have been made privy by the author to the various stages of Emma's development, it is extremely easy to forget that Mr. Knightley has not. *We* see Emma's misunderstanding of Harriet's feelings toward Frank and her tacit encouragement of a match between them; *we* see her subsequent discovery of her error, her mortification, her recognition of her love for Mr. Knightley, and her resolutions to reform. But Mr. Knightley sees none of this even after he has proposed and been accepted—precisely because Emma, in order to save both Harriet's face and her own, chooses not to tell him. Before the proposal he knows, of course, that she has repented both her plan to mate Harriet and Mr. Elton and her insult of Miss Bates at Box Hill, and he has been deeply pleased by that repentance. But these are only steps in Emma's development, not its culmination; about the great recognition scene in volume 3, chapter 11, which is one of the most decisive moments in her reformation, he knows nothing. Before the proposal he also hears her make the statement about Frank's attentions having flattered her vanity, but, as far as we can tell, he seems less aware of this as evidence of her growth in self-knowledge than as encouragement that he might be able to step into Frank's place. Thus, although Emma does become, in Wiesenfarth's words, "a lovable person" in the course of the action, there is no proof that Mr. Knightley wants to marry her "because" of this fact. Surprising though the suggestion may seem at first, he simply does not know enough about the extent of her reformation.

To understand his real motive, we have to look closely at the proposal scene itself. This has rarely been done, presumably because, as I suggested at the outset, we approach the scene in our reading with relaxed attention, expecting that it will be little more than a routine wind-up. One critic who has analyzed it in some detail is Babb, but his analysis does not touch on the question at hand.

At the beginning of the scene, we recall, Emma and Mr. Knightley are working radically at cross-purposes: he, having learned of Frank's engagement to Jane Fairfax and having assumed that it must be upsetting Emma, has hurried back from London "to soothe or to counsel her"; but she, unaware that he has heard the news, fears that he has come "to speak to her, of his attachment to Harriet." The dialogue which follows is shaped by these misunderstandings and falls into four phases. In the first (paragraphs 2–13) Mr. Knightley acts promptly on his purpose disclosing that he has heard of the engagement and by offering Emma consolation "in a tone of great sensibility." Emma, however, immediately perceives his misunderstanding and initiates the second phase of the scene (paragraphs 14–22) by revealing that she is not in love with Frank and never has been. Even though she admits that for a short time his attentions flattered her vanity, she asserts that she "'was somehow or other safe from him'" all along. Mr. Knightley, of course, is delighted to hear this. Not only, with his jealousy now removed, does he instantly revise his opinion of Frank's character, but, "in the momentary conquest of eagerness over judgment," he takes Emma's words as encouragement "that, in time, he might gain her affection himself." Thus, in the next phase of the scene (paragraphs 23–32), he begins to hint at this hope by speaking enviously of Frank's prospective marital happiness. Unfortunately, Emma interprets his remarks as hinting at a desire to marry Harriet, and, dreading to hear him declare his love for the girl, enjoins him to be silent. Mortified and crushed, he obeys. But then, realizing that she "could not bear to give him pain," Emma suddenly relents, and, though still imagining that he wishes to declare his love for Harriet, resolves to hear whatever he might have to say, and magnanimously invites him to speak. This invitation is the climactic turning-point in the whole scene; the fourth and last phase (paragraphs 33–38) follows immediately. For Mr. Knightley, misinterpreting her words as a sign that she understands his intention of declaring his love to her, and that she has suddenly become disposed to listen to him after all, can no longer contain his passion. True, Emma's representation of their relation as only a friendship is cooler and less encouraging than he would have liked, but it is better than the foregoing silence she imposed on him, and, besides, he has "'gone too far already for concealment.'" Accordingly, he proposes at once; Emma, after overcoming her stunned surprise, joyously accepts; and he attains to "something so like perfect happiness, that it could bear no other name."

It is clear, then, that Mr. Knightley's decision to marry Emma, far from being the result of cool deliberation, of a reasoned recognition and acceptance of her maturation, springs entirely from impulse. There is not the slightest suggestion in the scene that the proposal is contingent in any way upon his approval of her growth. Her declaration that she has never loved Frank and the seeming encouragement given to Mr. Knightley's hopes by her inviting him to speak are sufficient to release powerful emotions which have been pent up within him from the beginning of the scene, and which he can no longer control. Jane Austen, in fact, explicitly says as much: "He had come, in his anxiety to see how she bore Frank Churchill's engagement, with no selfish view, no view at all, but of endeavouring, if she allowed him an opening, to soothe or to counsel her. — *The rest had been the work of the moment, the immediate effect of what he heard, on his feelings*" (my italics). It follows, obviously, that if he had had any reason earlier to believe that she was not in love with Frank, and if she had seemed earlier to encourage him, he would have proposed just as readily then as now. Indeed, though in the course of the novel Emma becomes more "lovable" to the reader, for Mr. Knightley she has been "the sweetest and best of all creatures, *faultless in spite of all her faults*" (my italics) since at least her early adolescence, and he himself finally tells her this: "'I do not believe I did you any good. The good was all to myself, by making you an object of the tenderest affection to me. I could not think about you so much without doating on you, faults and all; and by dint of fancying so many errors, have been in love with you ever since you were thirteen at least.'" Thus, even if we allow for some degree of playful exaggeration here, the meaning of Mr. Knightley's words is patent: if Emma had only encouraged him, he would have proposed to her in the very first chapter of the book, before her moral development had even gotten under way! Instead of creating or augmenting his love, that moral development is relevant to Mr. Knightley's proposal only to the extent that it prompts his love to speak. By awakening from her self-deceptions — by discovering that she is not really cut out to be a spinster, as she had mistakenly thought at the beginning, and that it is Mr. Knightley whom she has loved all along, and not Frank — Emma is able for the first time to say those things in the proposal scene which unwittingly encourage Mr. Knightley's desire and lead him to believe (however faulty the evidence) that the opportune moment for revealing it has finally arrived. It is passion which spins the plot at this point, not reason. Far, then, from being "the least romantic" of Jane Austen's heroes, as Craik has called him, Mr. Knightley may perhaps be one of the most romantic of them all. At the very least, it is impossible to see him after this wonderfully comic and touching scene as anything but delightfully human.

Love: Surface and Subsurface

Juliet McMaster

I take the metaphor of my chapter title from Charlotte Brontë's memorable criticism of Jane Austen:

> She does her business of delineating the surface of the lives of genteel English people curiously well; there is a Chinese fidelity, a miniature delicacy in the painting: she ruffles her reader by nothing vehement, disturbs him by nothing profound: the Passions are perfectly unknown to her; she rejects even a speaking acquaintance with that stormy Sisterhood; . . . Her business is not half so much with the human heart as with the human eyes, mouth, hands and feet; what sees keenly, speaks aptly, moves flexibly, it suits her to study, but what throbs fast and full, though hidden . . . —*this* Miss Austen ignores.

It is the original and recurring objection to Jane Austen. Mark Twain (who apparently so missed violence in the novels that he thought she shouldn't have been allowed to die a natural death!), complained that her characters are automatons which can't "warm up and feel a passion." And even her admirers defended her in terms which to her detractors are damningly faint praise. George Henry Lewes announced, "First and foremost let Jane Austen be named, the greatest artist that has ever written, using the term to signify the most perfect mastery over the means to her end. There are heights and depths in human nature which Miss

From *Jane Austen on Love*. ©1978 by Juliet McMaster. University of Victoria, 1978.

Austen has never scaled nor fathomed, there are worlds of passionate existence into which she has never set foot; . . . Her circle may be restricted, but it is complete." Elizabeth Barrett Browning was all too ready to accept this view: the novels, she said, are "perfect as far as they go—that's certain. Only they don't go far, I think." "Perfect," for Mrs. as for Mr. Browning, is a term of opprobrium. It means the reach doesn't exceed the grasp.

In the twentieth century Jane Austen certainly does not want for discriminating critics who make large claims for her significance, but again we who are her admirers have taken our stand on her appeal to the head rather than the heart. Ian Watt quotes Horace Walpole's dictum that "this world is a comedy to those that think, a tragedy to those that feel," and acknowledges "Jane Austen's novels are comedies, and can have little appeal to those who, consciously or unconsciously, believe thought inferior to feeling." We have to a large extent conceded Charlotte Brontë's point, and agreed that Jane Austen's business is indeed with the head and not with the heart—we simply don't find her reaction as devastating a piece of criticism as she evidently meant it to be: valuing as we do the activity of the mind and the application of the intellect. We admire the unruffled surface, and have a properly Augustan reservation about the virtues of the kind of "vehemence" and "profundity" that Brontë misses. I myself have just been demonstrating Jane Austen's intellectual savouring of the love convention, and her affinities with Shakespearean comedy.

And yet . . . do we really need to concede as much as we do? In our heart of hearts (and I use the phrase designedly) don't we know that a *full* reading of a Jane Austen novel is a very *moving* experience, as well as an intellectually delectable one?—that the moment of reconciliation when Mr. Knightley *almost* kisses Emma's hand is fraught with passion, just as is the occasion when Mr. Rochester crushes Jane Eyre to his breast in the orchard at Thornfield, while a violent midsummer storm is brewing?

How is it done? Well, deep reservoirs may have unruffled surfaces as well as shallow ones: if unruffled surface is what we admire, then we need not look beyond it—and we can delight in the fidelity with which the surface of the lives of genteel English people is delineated; but if we do indeed value the dramatization of deep emotion, that too is there, and the more visible, if not the more obvious, for the apparent tranquillity.

Charlotte Brontë, accused on one occasion of equivocation, vindicated herself vigorously: "I would scorn in this and every other case to deal in equivoque; I believe language to have been given us to make our meaning clear, and not to wrap it in dishonest doubt." I suspect Jane Austen would consider such a declaration somewhat crude. The naïve Catherine Morland in *Northanger Abbey* has something similar to say of General Tilney's white lies: "Why he should say one thing so positively, and mean another all the while, was most unaccountable! How were people, at that rate, to be understood?" And Catherine's education is to involve the realization that language need not always be interpreted literally.

Of course novelists and dramatists have traditionally made capital out of a discrepancy between the profession and the reality, and many a comic scene has been built around it. Here is Becky Sharp, justifying herself to Jos Sedley when he has come to visit her in her disreputable lodgings: she has just stowed the brandy bottle, the rouge-pot, and the plate of broken meat in the bed.

> "I have had so many griefs and wrongs, Joseph Sedley, I have been made to suffer so cruelly, that I am almost made mad and sometimes. . . . I had but one child, one darling, one hope, one joy, which I held to my heart with a mother's affection . . . ; and they—they tore it from me—tore it from me;" and she put her hand to her heart with a passionate gesture of despair, burying her face for a moment on the bed.
>
> The brandy-bottle inside clinked up against the plate which held the cold sausage. Both were moved, no doubt, by the exhibition of so much grief.
>
> (*Vanity Fair*, chap. 65)

Becky pours out her wrongs and her griefs; the brandy-bottle and the rouge-pot tell a different story. Sometimes Thackeray even provides a direct translation of the subsurface meaning. In another memorable scene between the same pair, when they nervously await the event of Waterloo in Brussels, Becky tells Jos:

> "You men can bear anything. . . . Parting or danger are nothing to you. Own now that you were going to join the army and leave us to our fate. I know you were—something tells me you were. I was so frightened, when the thought came into my head (for I do sometimes think of you when I'm alone, Mr. Joseph!), that I ran off immediately to beg and entreat you not to fly from us."

> This speech might be interpreted, "My dear sir, should an accident befall the army, and a retreat be necessary, you have a very comfortable carriage, in which I propose to take a seat."
> (chap. 31)

I have indulged in this little digression on Becky Sharp because she provides a convenient contrast to the usual process in Jane Austen. Becky's speech is a gush of emotion; Becky's meaning is totally a product of that energetic brain of hers, and one can almost hear the whirr and click of a calculating machine in action. Jane Austen's characters, on the other hand, conduct apparently rational conversations with each other on subjects of general interest, while simultaneously their *hearts* are deeply engaged. She is not particularly interested in the exposure of the hypocrite who uses social forms as a mask for his true motivation. Nor is Charlotte Brontë, by the way—it is notable that in the proposal scene in *Jane Eyre* Jane declares explicitly, "I am not talking to you now through the medium of custom, [or] conventionalities" (chap. 23). Jane Eyre and Lucy Snowe have to maintain a proud reticence, or burst through the barriers of convention in order to express their feelings, and when they do burst through they mean all they say; Becky Sharp and Blanche Amory are socially perfectly at ease in the display of emotion, but they mean something different. But Jane Austen's characters succeed in expressing themselves not in spite of custom and convention, but *through* them; and they mean not something different from what they say, like Thackeray's, nor all they say, like Charlotte's, but far more than what they say. So when Elinor receives Edward after their estrangement, actually believing him to be married to Lucy Steele, we can gather enough of the agonized state of her feelings by hearing merely that "she sat down again and talked of the weather."

And here we come to her powerful use of understatement in emotional scenes. It is her frequent practice to bring a situation to a crisis, to lead you to the point where you expect some climactic exclamation of the "Great was her consternation . . . !" type, and then to report instead some apparent commonplace of behaviour or polite converse. There is a breath of a pause, a kind of hiatus between cause and effect (which I indicate typographically by a double stroke), that we learn to perceive and savour. "No sooner had Fatima discovered the gory remains of Bluebeard's previous wives, //than she made an appointment with her hairdresser"—I must invent a gross example to attune the ear and eye to Jane Austen's refined and delicate use of this device.

For instance:

Elizabeth Bennet has at last realized that Darcy is the man she loves, but just when she has come to believe that he will never approach her again. Her mother calls her to the window to see the arrival of Mr. Bingley. "Elizabeth, to satisfy her mother, went to the window—she looked,—she saw Mr. Darcy with him, and//sat down again by her sister."

Mary Crawford, in spite of her prejudice against younger brothers, has fallen in love with Edmund Bertram. She is engaged in a game of Speculation when the gentlemen's conversation turns on the eligibility of Thornton Lacey as a gentleman's residence: "Thornton Lacey was the name of [Edmund's] impending living, as Miss Crawford well knew; and//her interest in a negociation for William Price's knave increased."

Anne Elliot has steeled herself to speak to Mrs. Croft of her brother, Captain Wentworth, brave in the knowledge that Mrs. Croft knows nothing of the previous engagement:

> "Perhaps you may not have heard that he is married," added Mrs. Croft. [Anne]//could now answer as she ought.

Again and again Jane Austen indicates a severe emotional shock by this kind of understatement. She is not *avoiding* the presentation of strong feelings; she is presenting them by indirection. It is not because her characters have no feelings that they talk of the weather and make polite responses in such moments. Words would not carry the full weight of what they feel in any case. They observe the social forms, but not at the expense of crushing themselves. For what they feel they *can* express, but they can seldom express it directly or fully: to spill out the words and feelings, regardless of decorum, is to lose the intensity, to be emotionally shallow. (That is what Jane Austen tried to suggest in *Sense and Sensibility*, when Elinor hears the man she loves is married, and *Marianne* goes into hysterics.) Her people speak in a succinct code, where A expresses not only A, but B and C as well.

I would like to examine, in some detail, a . . . passage of dialogue, and to show how polite conversation, conducted on matters of apparently general import, and within the bounds of decorum, can be informed with a subsurface level of intense personal emotion. One thing is said on the surface; but below the surface are implied the individual's ecstasies and agonies. In this way I hope to mine some of that rich and primitive ore which Charlotte Brontë misses. . . .

> Here is [a] neglected girl who looks on while the man she loves pursues an unworthy woman; but . . . . the point of view is centered not in the neglected girl, but in the unworthy one—in the erring Emma, in fact. To get the full emotional impact of all that is going on in this novel, we must sometimes make the imaginative leap that is needed to understand what the restrained Jane Fairfax is feeling, for Emma herself is of course hot-headed but cool-hearted, and for most of the novel doesn't know her own feelings.

Few of us can fail to have been impressed by the extraordinary power of the Box Hill scene. Its power resides in the fact that beneath all that conversation and badinage, and beneath the over-strained attempt to make a party go, there are two subsurface levels of action, which the alert reader is aware of, and which give the surface level particular intensity. On one level, at least one of the principals is not aware of what is going on: Emma's unconscious love for Mr. Knightley is beginning to force itself to the surface of her mind, and makes her realize that "she felt less happy than she had expected. She laughed because she was disappointed." Frank Churchill suggests that for her entertainment everyone must reveal his thoughts; Mr. Knightley asks pointedly,

> "Is Miss Woodhouse sure that she would like to hear what we are all thinking of?"
>
> "Oh! no, no"—cried Emma, laughing as carelessly as she could—"Upon no account in the world."

Divided from Mr. Knightley by the "principle of separation" that prevails, and pointlessly incurring his disapprobation by her joyless flirting with Frank Churchill, she is weighed down by a misery she can't define. From this state of mind arises her cruel joke at Miss Bate's expense, followed by her ride home in the carriage with the unconcealed tears running down her face.

In the other action, the principals are thoroughly awake to the language of implication, and are aiming covert barbs at each other which they mean to strike and wound. Frank Churchill and Jane Fairfax, the secret lovers, have quarrelled, and his pointed attentions to Emma are designed to express to Jane his independence of her. He is under *Miss Woodhouse's* command; he implores *Miss Woodhouse* to choose and educate a wife for him, since he has no faith in his own choice. He and Jane proceed in their covert quarrel to break off their engagement. Frank says of the Eltons (who like himself and Jane met at a public watering-place) that they are "lucky" their marriage is as happy as it is. His apparently general comments are deeply insulting to Jane.

> "Very lucky—marrying as they did, upon an acquaintance formed only in a public place! . . . —for as to any real knowledge of a person's disposition that Bath, or any public place, can give—it is all nothing; there can be no knowledge. It is only by seeing women in their own homes, among their own set, just as they always are, that you can form any just judgment. Short of that, it is all guess and luck—and will generally be ill-luck. How many a man has committed himself on a short acquaintance, and rued it all the rest of his life!"

Jane Fairfax has her cue to answer: "A hasty and imprudent attachment may arise—but there is generally time to recover from it afterwards." "Jane," he can be understood to say—(I wish I could write the scene as Charlotte would have liked it; but then I like it the way it is)—"Jane, now that I've seen you in your sordid little home, with your dreary family, I'm thoroughly disillusioned, and I wish to God I hadn't got involved with you." "Frank," she may be supposed to reply, "get lost." At any rate, as Frank afterwards acknowledges, "She spoke her resentment in a form of words perfectly intelligible to me."

That form of words is not, I suspect, perfectly intelligible to Charlotte Brontë and her allies. She accused Jane Austen of being deaf to the rhythms of the human heart, but she herself had no ear for the still small voice. She was attuned to what Scott called "The Big Bow-wow strain."

In general terms I have been talking about the power of form to liberate rather than to limit. In art the restrictions of form and discipline do not confine, but rather *de*fine. "As well a well wrought urne becomes/The greatest ashes, as halfe-acre tombes"—the sentiment was shared and practised by Jane Austen, even if the metaphor would be hardly characteristic. Her novels are well wrought urns, where Charlotte Brontë's preference was more in the line of half-acre tombs. I have had occasion to quote Donne once before in this chapter; and, strange bedfellows as they seem at first sight, Donne and Jane Austen have much in common. They both have the conviction that it is not the quantity of experience that counts, but the quality; and they both have the concomitant power to make "one little roome, an every where." They find the world's room in a bed, in a relationship, or in Highbury, or in those "3 or 4 Families in a Country Village" that Jane Austen delighted in writing about.

We all know that Jane Austen was an ironist. Studies of her irony have formed the mainstay of much recent criticism of her novels. But we usually associate irony with the intellect: we think of it as a polemical tool, or as a means of creating comedy through its illumination of incongruity; we assume that the ironist maintains a cerebral detachment, like Mr. Bennet's in *Pride and Prejudice*. Marvin Mudrick even heads one of the chapters of his book on Jane Austen's irony "Irony and Convention *versus* Feeling." But irony and feeling are not necessarily opposed: there is an irony used to express emotion as well as an irony used to make fun of it. Arthur Sidgewick pointed this out in an early and illuminating article on the term: "It often comes about," he said, "that while the lower stages of feeling can be expressed, the higher stages must be suggested. In the ascent the full truth will do; but the climax can only be reached by irony." I do not claim quite this much for Jane Austen—she does not deal in the tragic experience of an Oedipus or an Othello; but her power of understatement, and ability to express feelings by indirection, inform her novels with emotional intensity. She offers us far more than the *surface* of the lives of genteel English people.

Civilization and the Contentment of *Emma*

Julia Prewitt Brown

There is a plaguing discrepancy, familiar to anyone who has written on *Emma*, between reading the novel and writing about it. The novel's first great strength lies in the ability to draw the reader in. We are made happy in the traps that are laid for us; we roll in their nets and sleep. We read, in the words of E. M. Forster, with mouth open and mind closed; and after we have finished the spell is broken. Then we can begin to think about it, when the remembered event and the inferred theme have lost their primary, exigent brilliance. The pleasure of reading *Emma*, the very great pleasure, has little to do with the kinds of linear meaning that may be found in most novels; the pleasure comes from our willing immersion in the everyday concerns and relationships of this world, and from a glow of suggestion in the narrative that tells us: this is enough. The novel's very self-absorption makes it acceptable and wonderful. It is a world that believes in itself entirely, and hypnotized, we too believe.

How is this irresistible self-absorption achieved and sustained? There are many answers to this question. One concerns the structure of the novel. Most novels written during the eighteenth and nineteenth-centuries, and even many later ones, are teleologically structured—either overtly, like *Pride and Prejudice* and *Great Expectations*, or ironically, like *Tom Jones* and *Vanity Fair*. To miss the outcome of these stories is to miss the meaning. This causal structure is not realized in a few exceptions, notably *Tristram Shandy* and *Emma*, whose conclusions are not, as

From *Jane Austen's Novels: Social Change and Literary Form*. Harvard University Press, 1979.

it were, judiciously weighted. Although we may wonder, like Mr. Knightley, what will become of Emma, her destiny, either social or moral, has little to do with her actions. She is not punished for her misconduct; she does not earn the perfect happiness that is hers in the end. Nor are we disturbed by the non sequitur; although she is often in error, we never feel she is heading toward any retribution except enlightenment. Emma's fate does not identify her the way, say, Isabel Archer's fate makes her Isabel Archer. Emma is always Emma, an integrated, functioning whole; after all her surprises and self-criticism, we still enjoy her in the same way. When she says near the close of the novel, "Oh! I always deserve the best treatment, because I never put up with any other," we smile at her once again, or perhaps with her. Lionel Trilling calls this structure "forgiving," yet the idea of forgiveness still assumes a causal plot. That Emma is never properly humbled by fate has little to do with pride forgiven, but is a matter of personal being. Because she is Emma, acting out her extraordinary nature from beginning to end, we are satisfied. Our *not* thinking about matters of forgiveness is what makes our immersion in her concerns so effortless.

Just as the structure of *Emma* is not causal, it is also not hierarchical. Were we to draw a picture of the novel, it would not, I believe, bring before the reader the ladder of social and moral being that Graham Hough assigns. It would look more like a road map in which the cities and towns, joined together by countless highways and byroads, stood for people. Some of the roads are curved and smooth, like those between Emma and her father or Emma and Mrs. Weston; some are so full of obstacles that their destinations (Jane Fairfax, for example) are almost inaccessible. Mr. Weston and Miss Bates are like great indiscriminate towns from which radiate roads that join almost everyone.

As the image of a road map suggests, Highbury is a system of interdependence, a community of people all talking to one another, affecting, and changing one another: a collection of relationships. Miss Bates is emblematic of Highbury in this respect. In the words of E. M. Forster, "Miss Bates is bound by a hundred threads to Highbury. We cannot tear her away without bringing her mother too, and Jane Fairfax and Frank Churchill, and the whole of Box Hill." Emma herself is as firmly connected to her world as Miss Bates. Perceived in her many relationships with others, Emma is seen as daughter, sister, sister-in-law, aunt, companion, intimate friend, new acquaintance, patroness, and bride. And each connection lets us see something new in her.

The interaction of characters in the novel is extensive and dynamic.

All characters intersect in some way. In addition to all the major combinations, we witness sufficiently realized contact between Jane Fairfax and Mr. John Knightley, Mr. Weston and Mrs. Elton, Mr. Elton and Mr. John Knightley; we learn what Mr. Woodhouse thinks of Frank Churchill, what Mr. John Knightley thinks of Mr. Weston, and what Isabella thinks of Harriet. These represent brief encounters and the almost spur-of-the-moment judgments that arise from them. For example, Mr. John Knightley has only to see Mr. Elton once during his holiday visit to know that Mr. Elton is interested in Emma. As always in Jane Austen, the smallest detail of behavior can justify the most definitive judgment.

Even the more sustained relationships seem to be composed of many individual encounters and the individual judgments that arise from them. For example, the relationships between Mrs. Elton and Jane Fairfax, Frank Churchill and his foster parents, Jane Fairfax and Emma, and Harriet and Robert Martin's sister are discussed several times by different persons, and on the basis of brief incidents. When compared to the pattern of dialogue in *Pride and Prejudice*, these dialogues and judgments seem random and self-absorbed—indeed, like "real" conversations—yet not the less reliable for being so. Mr. Woodhouse's judgment upon Frank Churchill—that the young man is "not quite the thing"—is unreasonably and uncharitably founded, yet correct; and it is acknowledged with dismay by those who hear it.

The novel is like Highbury itself; there is no limit to the combinations within it, or to the combinations speculated upon. Marriage, always the first and last relationship in Jane Austen, is confirmed in six couples in the novel and predicted in many more. (Harriet and Mr. Elton, Emma and Mr. Elton, Emma and Frank Churchill, Harriet and Frank Churchill, Jane Fairfax and Mr. Dixon, Mr. Knightley and Jane Fairfax, Harriet and Mr. Knightley.) Indeed, speculation about love relationships is the basis of the novel's plot, because the heroine is herself a relentless matchmaker. Yet to catalogue all of these real or imagined connections is misleading. In its unlikely and changing combinations, the catalogue gives an impression of social irrationality, overworked variety, and exhaustive socialization. Yet no other novel has more the opposite effect: of rich, unbroken continuity, of uncluttered awareness, routine contentment, cooperation, and harmony. This effect is achieved not only because of the interdependence of Highbury, its commune-like nature, but because events and characters are likened to one another in subtle ways, like so many hues of one color. This too helps to explain the magic and magnetic appeal of *Emma*; we are transfixed by the kaleidoscopic patterning of its relationships.

The similarities between Emma and Mrs. Elton are often noted. Both are preoccupied with status; each adopts another young woman as protégée and satellite; both are self-centered and therefore blind. Jane Fairfax and Emma also are compared and contrasted; Miss Bates is Jane's Mr. Woodhouse. Miss Taylor is to Emma what Emma plans to be to Harriet. Mr. Perry has his counterpart in town, Mr. Wingfield. And so on.

The similarities always have psychological meaning. Characters have a tendency to repeat the relationships they have known; for example, Emma seeks a replacement for Mrs. Weston in Harriet. Isabella Knightley finds her Mr. Perry in town, another doctor who like his counterpart parodically embodies the atavistic, maternal relationship founded on one-sided knowledge and care. Both Jane Fairfax and Frank Churchill are orphaned; their original relationships disrupted, neither has a secure prototype to follow. It is difficult for Jane Fairfax to connect with others; she feels far more isolated in the presence of her aunt, for example, than Emma does in the presence of her father. Frank, on the other hand, has no notion at all of what a relationship is, of reciprocal endeavor and trust. Unlike Jane's unwavering attachment to him, his love does not include loyalty—he not only flirts with Emma but does so to torment his fiancée. Since neither has received the education of a steady and lasting parental relationship, as Emma has, they can only form an attachment that becomes "a source of repentance and misery to each." (Because of the unvalidated status of their relationship their marriage is left waiting at the end of the novel.)

Many of the transformations, actions, and events in *Emma* take place in the form of repetitions. Emma has three enlightenments; related respectively to Mr. Elton, Frank Churchill, and Mr. Knightley, they increase in intensity yet are essentially similar. Isolated events are also replayed in a changed key; Mr. Knightley rescues Harriet at the Crown Ball in a scene of great romantic delicacy involving Emma; the next day Frank Churchill rescues Harriet from the gypsies in a burlesque version. The crudeness of the second event drowns out the delicacy of the first and prepares the way for Emma's wanton blow at Miss Bates at Box Hill. The ball scene in which Mr. Knightley performs his wonderfully unobtrusive act of kindness reverberates with suggestion. It brings Emma and Mr. Knightley together for the first time; it joins them through an act of charity in the way Emma earlier planned to join Mr. Elton and Harriet the day they visited the cottage. And the look of approval Emma sends across the dance floor that night is later matched by his silent expression of approval for Emma when she visits Miss Bates the morning after Box Hill. The most resonant instance of transformation as repetition in Jane Austen, of course, is marriage. The three marriages that close the novel are different yet similar, repetitive of one another and of the marriages in the beginning of the novel. The rich overlay of experience, the almost Shakespearean imaginative continuity of the novel, is all but hypnotizing.

Because *Emma* is a novel about relationships and their natures, the "action" of the work is a dialectic. Every relationship in the novel has its unique dialectical rhythm; even the smoothest relationships encounter snags, such as the near-argument between Mr. Woodhouse and Emma about the treatment of brides. The novel's humor is almost always centered on the surprise creation of a dialectic through the sudden juxtaposition of unlikely personalities. The conversation between Mr. Knightley and Mrs. Elton about the picnic at Donwell Abbey, one of the most amusing exchanges in English fiction, does not perform at all; the humor lies in the contrast of character and is available to those who see it. Such moments border on farce because of the deadly seriousness of the characters themselves. And Mr. Knightley, the most serious of all, is not exempted from the farce of the situation; the contrast is not available to his subjective standpoint.

Three major dialectics in the novel involve Emma herself: the interior dialectic, of which only Emma is aware; the dialectic between Emma and Mr. Knightley; and the dialectic between Emma and Highbury. By the close of the novel they all seem to become the same dialectic. They are never resolved, only validated, in marriage; the only truth is the dialectic itself. Part of the novel's greatness is that it never moves to the death of total resolution.

Emma's personality opens like a fan before us. Seen in her innumerable relationships with others, she alters continually and gracefully, and the novel is deliberately paced to allow this. Mr. Woodhouse's daughter is not Harriet's patroness or Mr. John Knightley's sister-in-law. The Emma who condescends to Harriet, self-satisfied, smirking, and dictatorial, is not the Emma we see with Mr. Knightley, witty, open, and daring. And although she is tied by countless social relations, she is neither overshadowed nor borne down by them. We cannot think of her as we do some nineteenth-century heroines, changing under circumstances like Darwinian organisms. Emma's inner nature, her stability as Emma, even as she is drawn this way and that—spoiled, criticized, disappointed, insulted, and loved—never alters; she is still Emma. Protean, elusive, capable of true goodness and deliberate cruelty, she is what she is—a reservoir of indeterminacy. She represents the genuine triumph of volition, for she is free to be better than she knows herself to be. She is faultless not in spite of her faults, but because of them.

Always doing "more than she wished and less than she ought," Emma is frequently divided between two impulses in her interior dialogue. There is a struggle, but never a war. In questioning her own treatment of the Martins, of Harriet, of Jane Fairfax, and of Miss Bates, she has some unsettling moments, yet her disposition is to like and accept herself wholeheartedly. Even after her most crucial, most soul-searching enlightenment, her final admission of her despicable treatment of Harriet, she swings back to a tolerably self-supporting state of mind. At length she begins to learn to treat others as generously as she treats herself, to accept the faultlessness of human interactions in spite of their faults. Emma's interior struggle is never laid to rest; the only resolution consists in trying to be better: "the only source whence anything like consolation or composure could be drawn, was in the resolution of her own better conduct." She never ceases to be one Emma and begins to be another.

Mr. Knightley, in his relation to Emma, takes the side of her that does or should do what she "ought." When she paints Harriet taller than she really is, only Mr. Knightley and this side of Emma acknowledge that she is doing it. Mr. Knightley seems to bring out the best in Emma; he makes her defend her right to be Emma, and in defending it, she becomes witty and challenging. "I shall not scold you. I leave you to your own reflections," says Mr. Knightley. "Can you trust me with such flatterers?" replies Emma. The tension between Emma and Mr. Knightley is as vital as that in a love affair in a novel by D. H. Lawrence. From their first words to each other, every encounter between them vibrates with their unique awareness of one another, their mutual knowledge disguised under apparent differences: "'You have made her too tall, Emma,' said Mr. Knightley. Emma knew that she had, but would not own it." And the secret knowledge of the other's character is not limited to Mr. Knightley. When he arrives at the Coles', Emma can tell he has come in his carriage and says:

> "There is always a look of consciousness or bustle when people come in a way which they know to be beneath them. You think you carry it off very well, I dare say, but with you it is a sort of bravado, an air of affected unconcern; I always

> it whenever I meet you under those circumstances. *Now* you have nothing to try for. You are not afraid of being supposed ashamed. You are not striving to look taller than any body else. *Now* I shall be very happy to walk in the same room with you."
>
> "Nonsensical girl!" was his reply, but not at all in anger.

Such encounters suggest an immediacy of awareness and intimacy that is undeniably sexual. There are no sexual "overtones" in *Emma*; the sexuality is there, in the minds and speech and emotional intensity of the characters, in the mental urgency of every encounter. The scene at the Crown Ball when Mr. Knightley asks the defenseless and snubbed Harriet to dance is alive with the sense of a new understanding between Emma and Mr. Knightley. Until the end of the chapter, no words are spoken between them; like the love in *Persuasion*, their love is silent. Eye contact replaces speech: "her countenance said much, as soon as she could catch his eye again." And the wonderfully powerful: "her eyes invited him irresistibly to come to her and be thanked." One feels that this is what being in love is about, not all the talk, planning, and invention Emma imagines it is. It is the power to move, to know the other person.

The Crown Ball is a scene of extraordinary delicacy and love. Set off by the benevolent hum of Miss Bates's monologue, its strength lies in Emma's watching Mr. Knightley perform this act of kindness; her appreciation of it makes her a better Emma than the Emma who mistreats the Martins, the Emma who is above everyone. And Mr. Knightley, who would do what he does now for any woman in the novel, does it here for Emma, as they both know. The dialogue that follows registers the new intimacy with spirit, and without losing a sense of their individuality. The scene ends in dance:

> "Will you?" said he, offering his hand.
>
> "Indeed I will. You have shown that you can dance, and you know we are not really so much brother and sister as to make it at all improper."
>
> "Brother and sister! no, indeed."

Mr. Knightley knows he loves Emma at this point; characteristically, Emma does not yet know she loves him. But the reader is not ignorant and his knowledge gives the scene its exquisite emotion.

The scene is surrounded and intertwined with contrasts that set off its romantic delicacy. Preceded by Mr. Weston's indiscriminate hospitality, Frank Churchill's nervousness, and the Eltons' sneering self-importance, Mr. Knightley's act suddenly crystallizes the three concerned—himself, Harriet, and Emma—in a brilliant tableau. Miss Bates's interpolated monologue is a wonderful contrast to the delicate discriminations of the event. It is as though their love were founded in her jumbled benevolence.

The chapter itself is framed on one side by Emma's private admission of an entirely deflated interest in Frank Churchill, and on the other by Frank Churchill's mock-heroic rescue of Harriet, pointedly used to establish the real heroism of Mr. Knightley's action. The ball scene in *Emma* is flanked by events that, through contrasts, set off its intensity and validate its sincerity.

It seems to me that in this respect *Emma* is a great novel about "the association of man and woman"—to use T. S. Eliot's phrase. Emma and Mr. Knightley actually make each other larger, more interesting. Without Mr. Knightley, Emma is a self-satisfied busy-body; without Emma, Mr. Knightley is a dull and predictable English gentleman. Emma is responsible for Mr. Knightley's one unpredictable act in the entire novel, his standing up Mr. Elton one morning. Infuriated, Mr. Elton recalls: "I met William Larkins . . . as I got near the house, and he told me I should not find his master at home, but I did not believe him.—William seemed rather out of humour. He did not know what was come of his master lately, he said." Because each has always possessed a part of the other, the marriage between Emma and Mr. Knightley does not wrench either from an old identity into a new one. They do not seek to annihilate one another—the way, for example, part of Edmund Bertram is annihilated when he marries Fanny. Emma is still Emma and Mr. Knightley still Mr. Knightley; Emma even wishes to continue to call him so. The only real difference is the knowledge of love between them, and the willingness to be influenced by the other that, as always, is central to Jane Austen's conception of love. After reading Mr. John Knightley's response to his brother's announcement of his engagement, Emma says:

> "He writes like a sensible man . . . I honour his sincerity. It is very plain that he considers the good fortune of the engagement as all on my side . . ."
>
> "My Emma, he means no such thing. He only means . . ."
>
> "He and I should differ very little in our estimation of the two,"—interrupted she, with a sort of serious smile—"much less, perhaps, than he is aware of . . ."

> "Emma, my dear Emma—"
>
> "Oh!" she cried with more thorough gaiety, "if you fancy your brother does not do me justice, only wait till my dear father is in the secret, and hear his opinion. Depend upon it, he will be much farther from doing *you* justice."

Here is the old Emma, asserting herself with the same archness and self-love, yet this time, with something new added—a kind of self-irony. "Oh! I always deserve the best treatment, because I never put up with any other."

Each wishes to make the other more like his or her self; yet each loves that part of the other that is not similar. This rapport between Emma and Mr. Knightley is, I believe, more central to the novel than Graham Hough's hierarchy of characters. Hough distinguishes five kinds of discourse in the novel and asserts that the "objective narrative" with its Johnsonian vocabulary and thoughtful, well-ordered, analytical generalizing sets "the standard by which all the rest is measured." Since Mr. Knightley's speech assimilates the objective narrative most completely, he is the highest on an unequivocal moral scale: "Mr. Knightley, who is never wrong, maintains this style of sober moral evaluation more consistently than anyone else. . . . In his presence, conversation is always lifted from the familiar and the anecdotal to the level of general reflection; the characters become types; and the actual persons around him assume the air of personae in a moral apologue." Hough gives as an example Mr. Knightley's comments concerning Mrs. Elton and Jane Fairfax: "Another thing must be taken into consideration too—Mrs. Elton does not talk to Miss Fairfax as she speaks of her. We all know the differences between the pronouns he or she and thou, the plainest spoken amongst us; we all feel the influence of something beyond common civility in our personal intercourse with each other—a something more early implanted. . . . And besides the operation of this as a general principle you may be sure that Miss Fairfax awes Mrs. Elton by her superiority both of mind and manner; and that face to face Mrs. Elton treats her with all the respect which she has a claim to." Yet Mr. Knightley's words simply are not true in the very example Hough gives. Mrs. Elton is irrepressible, so much so that she almost usurps the closing lines of the novel. Although we never see her alone with Jane Fairfax, we know from the liberties taken in finding Jane a position that Mrs. Elton's private behavior is as bold and intrusive as her public behavior. If Mrs. Elton is not awed by the "superiority both of mind and manner" of Mr. Knightley, who as Hough says is superior to all, she will not be awed by

Jane Fairfax. Mr. Knightley is wrong in his evaluation here, as he is in his optimistic insistence that, were Frank Churchill to act more virtuously toward his father, his foster parents would bend and respect him for it. Mr. Knightley is a pastoral figure who insists on seeing the "actual persons" around him as "personae in a moral apologue." This is not the way Jane Austen views the world, nor can it be the vision she really supports. As Mary Ellmann has said, the endorsement of moral stolidity is reluctant, qualified by Mr. Knightley's pleasure in Emma's defects: "I am losing all my bitterness against spoilt children, my dearest Emma. I who am owing all my happiness to *you*, would it not be horrible ingratitude in me to be severe on them?" The weight of the novel is centered not in Mr. Knightley but in Emma, or in the contributing tension between them.

Mr. Knightley is the link between Emma's interior struggle and her struggle with Highbury. He seems to represent both her conscience and the community. Almost every time Emma sets herself against her conscience, she is also setting herself against Mr. Knightley and against the values of Highbury. (Her treatment of Robert Martin is the best example of this opposition.) Emma's interior coordination, her quest to know and approve of herself, is solidly linked to her exterior coordination, or her arrival at a juster relation to others and to the community.

Essays on *Emma* have a tendency to describe Highbury the way an ethnographer writes history, sorting through the picked bones of institutions and beliefs. The inner consistency, the living society, escapes attention. Class divisions and difficulties are stressed, and moral traits are eventually viewed as possessions of a particular class, or class attitude. I do not intend to decry this view, but pursued too far, it reduces the society of Highbury to a sack of struggling types in some manner creating order out of chaos. It is not the Highbury Emma sees standing on the doorstep of Ford's one morning:

> Mr. Perry walking hastily by, Mr. William Cox letting himself in at the office door, Mr. Cole's carriage horses returning from exercise, or a stray letter-boy on an obstinate mule, were the liveliest objects she could presume to expect; and when her eyes fell only on the butcher with his tray, a tidy old woman travelling homewards from shop with her full basket, two curs quarrelling over a dirty bone, and a string of dawdling children round the baker's little bow-window eyeing the gingerbread, she knew she had no reason to complain and was amused enough; quite enough still to stand at the door.

Highbury, it is true, is made up of classes and their individual members. Yet however different the traits of personality and class, they are taken into a functioning society and reshaped by inner organizing forces. Miss Bates is perhaps the nearest symbol of Highbury; all classes join and cooperate in her, just as all gossip passes through her vacant mind. She is the repository of all that occurs and has occurred in Highbury. Her small apartment joins the older gentry (the Woodhouses and Knightleys), the new rich (the Coles), and the lower-middle to lower-class townspeople and clerks. She represents Highbury's fluidity and mobility, its tolerance of past and future classes, or part of the sensibility that helped England avoid a French Revolution.

Emma sets herself against this Highbury, as she does finally against Miss Bates at Box Hill. After every disagreement with Mr. Knightley she visits Miss Bates, as though humbly paying deference to Highbury itself. She does not like visiting Miss Bates for the very reason she should visit her: because it sanctions class fluidity. She does not wish to fall in with the "second and third rate of Highbury"; she wishes to have her own "set." Her greatest sin in the novel is cutting off Harriet's warm attachment to the Martins; as Lionel Trilling has said, she is a reactionary, out to stop social mobility. And Jane Austen gives her snobbery deliberately vindictive overtones: "The regular and best families Emma could hardly suppose [the Coles] would presume to invite—neither Donwell, nor Hartfield, nor Randalls. Nothing should tempt her to go, if they did; and she regretted that her father's known habits would be giving her refusal less meaning than she could wish." If anything saves Emma after such deliberate unkindness, it is that she actually wants to, and does, go to the Coles' dinner. At bottom, Emma is the most social person in the novel: totally preoccupied with and loving all her relationships with people. This is the basis of the contrast between her and Jane Fairfax, who is a solitary, and who, in her marriage to a morally and intellectually inferior person, will continue to be a solitary.

One of the many ironies surrounding Emma's social preferences is that she will not admit the "true gentility" of Robert Martin, documented by the simple dignity of his written proposal to Harriet and his behavior to her after she refuses him, and yet will sit through an evening of "everyday remarks, dull repetitions, old news, and heavy jokes" at the Coles' and decide them to be "worthy people, who deserved to be made happy." The reason for the contradiction lies in the conclusion to this quotation: "And left a name behind that would not soon die away." What Emma requires of her inferior acquaintances is that they aggrandize her. In her comment about Robert Martin she makes this

:lear: "The yeomanry are precisely the order of people with whom I feel can have nothing to do. A degree or two lower, and a creditable ap- earance might interest me; I might hope to be useful to their families in ome way or other. But a farmer can need none of my help, and is there- ore in one sense as much above my notice as in every other he is below t." And we see the self-serving nature of her patronage of the lower-class vhen she visits the sick cottager.

Emma's charity visit has undergone many interpretations, and lmost always appears in any discussion of Jane Austen's class attitudes. n trying to answer the question of *Emma*'s relevance to us today, Arnold Kettle points out that it is not necessary for a novelist writing in Jane usten's time to suggest a solution to the problem of class divisions and rejudice, but that it is morally necessary for the author to notice the ex- tence of the problem. Jane Austen, he decides, fails to do so:

> The values and standards of the Hartfield world are based on the assumption that it is right and proper for a minority of the community to live at the expense of the majority. No amount of sophistry can get away from this fact and to discuss the moral concern of Jane Austen without facing it would be hypocrisy. It is perfectly true that, within the assumptions of aristocratic society, the values recommended in *Emma* are sensitive enough. Snobbery, smugness, condescension, lack of consideration, unkindness of any description, are held up to our disdain. But the fundamental condescension, the basic unkindness which permits the sensitive values of *Emma* to be applicable only to one person in ten or twenty, is this not left unscathed? Is there not here a complacency which renders the hundred little incomplacencies almost irrelevant?

'his is highly persuasive criticism of *Emma*, and Kettle is right in saying 1at "no amount of sophistry" can disguise the fundamental questions it aises. Yet it persuades us mainly because the writer is so sure of his noral stance—most literary criticism is far more slippery—and because hat stance happens to be a particularly appealing one. The moral judg- nent made against *Emma* is disturbingly simple. First of all, there are no aristocrats" in the novel; even the Churchills are just inflated gentry. Nor does Jane Austen view the landed class in the novel as parasitic; she ees it as a functioning part of a changing organism. Mr. Knightley nanages his land, has little cash, and has a younger brother who makes a living as a lawyer. Emma's destiny as a woman—to be spoiled, over- protected, given a weak, trivial education, and then left to her own devices—is hardly to be envied. And the social world of the novel is peopled with upwardly and downwardly mobile individuals. It is viewed not from the perspective of frozen class division but from a perspective of living change. It is not France in the 1780s but England at the beginning of the nineteenth century.

Kettle's interpretation of the scene of Emma's visit to the sick cottager forms the basis of his argument; it is in this particular scene that the moral issue is "shelved," that the existence of the problem is unrecognized. Yet while he notes the irony of Emma's remarks upon leaving the cottage, his conclusions rest exclusively upon the visit and its aftermath. Emma's words before she arrives at the cottage are equally significant. Having told Harriet she will never marry, Emma explains why her own spinsterhood could never make her ridiculous:

> Never mind, Harriet, I shall not be a poor old maid; and it is poverty only which makes celibacy contemptible to a generous public! A single woman, with a very narrow income, must be a ridiculous, disagreeable, old maid! the proper sport of boys and girls; but a single woman, of good fortune, is always respectable, and may be as sensible and pleasant as anybody else. And the distinction is not quite so much against the candour and common sense of the world as appears at first; for a very narrow income has a tendency to contract the mind, and sour the temper. Those who can barely live, and who live perforce in a very small, and generally very inferior, society, may well be illiberal and cross.

The exaggerated expressions and conceited ironies of Emma's speech are characteristic of her conversation in Harriet's company. If Mr. Knightley's skepticism makes her witty, Harriet's servile awe makes her unreasonable. When asked, as they near the cottage, if she knows Jane Fairfax, Emma replies:

> Oh! yes; we are always forced to be acquainted whenever she comes to Highbury. By the bye, *that* is almost enough to put one out of conceit with a niece. Heaven forbid! at least, that I should ever bore people half so much about all the Knightleys together, as she does about Jane Fairfax. One is sick of the very name of Jane Fairfax. Every letter from her is read forty times over; her compliments to all friends go round and round again; and if she does but send her aunt the pattern of a stomacher, or knit a pair of garters for her grandmother, one hears

> of nothing else for a month. I wish Jane Fairfax very well; but she tires me to death.

The poverty that Emma speaks of in the first quotation and the sickness she feels in hearing about Jane Fairfax find their counterparts in the real "sickness and poverty . . . which she came to visit." The contempt Emma really feels for the poor is very clear in the first speech (poor and elderly spinsters are "the proper sport of boys and girls"); her willingness to allow them to be "illiberal and cross" is an extension of her contempt. In the cottage this attitude is elaborated: "She understood their ways, could allow for their ignorance and their temptations, had no romantic expectations of extraordinary virtue from those, for whom education had done so little." Emma's "allowance" for ignorance and temptation is no more than an assumption of them. Even after reading Robert Martin's letter, we recall, she still insists that he is ignorant. The snapping bitterness of her tirade against Jane Fairfax, who is less fortunate than herself and who will have to earn a living, is enough to prove that even the rich can be illiberal and cross: "One is sick of the very name of Jane Fairfax . . . I wish Jane Fairfax very well; but she tires me to death." When such an example of Emma's compassion is followed with "They were now approaching the cottage, and all idle topics were superseded. Emma was very compassionate," the irony is so obvious that I question Kettle's interpretation that the moral issue is being shelved. The self-satisfied feeling Emma derives from the visit culminates when, upon seeing Mr. Elton, she says, "Well, (smiling) I hope it may be allowed that if compassion has produced exertion and relief to the sufferers, it has done all that is truly important. If we feel for the wretched, enough to do all we can for them, the rest is empty sympathy, only distressing to ourselves." Once again, the reappearance of a single word, in this case "distressing," makes us aware of the gap between Emma's real and spoken intentions. Even the "distresses of the poor" finally disappear into "what is distressing to ourselves."

It is precisely the moral issue then that is being put forward, put forward on the most demanding level: the practical, individual level. What is being subordinated to it is the collective issue, or the theoretical view of conduct as an expression of class. Such a view would let Emma off the hook, would make her class more responsible for her attitude than her own being. For all Jane Austen's awareness of the effect of class on character, she is never naïve enough to overlook the existence of individual volition. She would not have written off the "little incomplacencies" as readily as Kettle dces. To Austen's view, the "hundred little incomplacencies" make life tolerable for everyone; are we not required to imagine the effects of Emma's complacency on Robert Martin and his family? Emma is wrong to snub the Martins, and to encourage Harriet to snub them, not because as a class the yeomanry deserve to rise, but because she aims to break a moral and emotional tie between Harriet and the Martins that has already formed. It is on this level, the level of individual practice, that social damage is incurred in Jane Austen. From this point of view Kettle's broad class complacency is an abstraction, an evasion. Changes in the quality of social life originate on the concrete, atomized level.

Emma herself learns this lesson in the course of the novel. Indeed, it is her first lesson, because until she recognizes her own immediate effect on others, on Harriet and the Martins and Miss Bates, until she actually experiences her tie to a community of others, all talk about social responsibility and class difference is lost on her. In *Emma*, Austen makes us see the primary obstacles to class consciousness.

Emma's feelings toward her social inferiors are governed not so much by an unwillingness to see, converse with, or help them as by an insistence on regulating their lives. She does not wish to participate in Highbury society unless she can lead, on the dance floor and elsewhere. In essence she wishes not to cooperate but to rule, as Frank Churchill's mock proclamations at Box Hill suggest. Miss Bates offends her because she is uncontrollable; Emma cannot stop or even regulate the flow of her boring remarks. The urge to control is the basis of her insult at Box Hill: Miss Bates's dull remarks must be "limited as to number—only three at once."

It is important to Emma to feel that Highbury needs her but that she does not need Highbury. She imagines herself the envy and idol of all her social inferiors: young Robert Martin "will connect himself well if he can"; and the Coles' main object in giving the dinner is to see Emma at their table. At every social event Emma sees herself as giving the honor rather than as possibly receiving it. E. M. Forster's remark is appropriate to her: for some, it is perhaps better to receive than to give.

Emma's unwillingness to mix with Highbury has a personal analogue in her wish to remain single. Both reveal the same superior tendency to remain aloof, to oversee life without participating in it. Her first realization of love is appropriately attended by the first realization of her need for human society generally:

> The child to be born at Randall's must be a tie there even dearer than herself; and Mrs. Weston's heart and time would

> be occupied by it. They should lose her; and, probably, in great measure, her husband also.—Frank Churchill would return among them no more; and Miss Fairfax, it was reasonable to suppose, would soon cease to belong to Highbury. They would be married, and settled either at or near Enscombe. All that were good would be withdrawn; and if to these losses, the loss of Donwell were to be added, what would remain of cheerful or of rational society within their reach? Mr. Knightley to be no longer coming there for his evening comfort!—No longer walking in at all hours, as if ever willing to change his own home for their's!—How was it to be endured?

A great deal of the force of Emma's realization of love lies in the implicit recognition of dependence, of need, for another person. What astounds her is her own failure to see, year after year, the importance of Mr. Knightley's presence to her.

And once the love and need for another person is admitted, a sense of obligation naturally follows. It is significant that Emma achieves knowledge of her "heart" and knowledge of her "conduct" simultaneously: "It darted through her, with the speed of an arrow, that Mr. Knightley must marry no one but herself! . . . Her own conduct, as well as her own heart, was before her in the same few minutes. She saw it all with a clearness which had never blessed her before. How improperly had she been acting by Harriet! How inconsiderate, how indelicate, how irrational, how unfeeling had been her conduct! What blindness, what madness, had led her on!" Emma learns a "sense of justice" for the first time—in the words of *Mansfield Park*, a sense of "what is owed to everybody." Never in Jane Austen do we find a convenient separation between the personal and the social act. As Mr. Knightley tells Emma at Box Hill, her remark to Miss Bates--to Emma no more than a careless indulgence—is inevitably a public act: "You, whom she had known from an infant, whom she had seen grow up from a period when her notice was an honour, to have you now, in thoughtless spirits, and the pride of the moment, laugh at her, humble her—and before her niece, too—and before others, many of whom (certainly *some*) would be entirely guided by *your* treatment of her."

The scene at Box Hill possesses great emotional intensity. Each time we read it—no matter how objective familiarity or reason may have made us—Emma's cruelty completely shocks us. There is something particularly moving and frightening about the rejection of the comic figure in art, such as the rejection of Falstaff or of a clown in a Charlie Chaplin film. Miss Bates's emotional vulnerability, her blind (indeed her comic) goodness in expecting others to be as simply affectionate as herself, gives the scene its special pathos. And however Mr. Knightley finally stresses Miss Bates's social vulnerability, his speech begins with the frankly appalled question, "How could you be so unfeeling to Miss Bates?"

Yet the lack of feeling is not what makes the scene so shocking. Emma's action violates the most basic human law found in any society whether barbarous or advanced: the protection of the weak. Miss Bates is defenseless, as the first description of her makes clear: "She had not intellectual superiority to make atonement to herself, or to frighten those who might hate her, into outward respect." What leads Emma to mistreat her? We cannot really answer this question any more than we can explain an act of violence in an absurdist work. It is hot; Emma is tired of herself and of Frank Churchill; she is bored; and her discontent flowers with terrifying naturalness into cruelty.

Emma delivers the insult because she "could not resist." And the remarkable impact of the scene comes from our understanding her action though we know it to be wrong. We understand it not through its overt causes—Emma's impatience and boredom, her exasperated attempt to entertain herself since no one else will entertain her—but through its covert reality: there is no reason for it; it is simply a case of unrestrained human hostility. In this moment, perhaps more than in any other moment in Jane Austen, it is impossible to entertain D. W. Harding's notion of the "social detachment" that arises from having to restrain ourselves in society; indeed, only through restraint do the characters achieve a modicum of "social engagement." It is through resisting these irresistible impulses and hostilities that people in Austen's society can maintain a tolerably open atmosphere for the individual. Where, finally, do Emma's "honesty" and "sincerity" place Miss Bates but in a condition of social estrangement? Emma's famous cruelty takes place in the open air of Box Hill (itself a contradiction in terms), in a "natural" environment away from the home community. This choice of setting gives us a rather pointed indication of Jane Austen's opinion of human nature, of how human beings behave when the muzzle is off. To Jane Austen, nothing boxes the individual in more tightly than his own craving for freedom.

Unlike Emma, Mr. Knightley has, in his own words, the "English delicacy toward the feelings of other people," as his protection of the slow-witted and defenseless Harriet reveals. In his conversation with Mrs. Elton, Mr. Knightley states his understanding of human behavior, and we observe one of the most richly ambivalent problems in Jane Austen realizing itself.

> "It is to be a morning scheme, you know, Knightley; quite a simple thing. I shall wear a large bonnet, and bring one of my little baskets hanging on my arm. Here,—probably this basket with pink ribbon. And Jane will have such another. There is to be no form or parade—a sort of gipsy party.—We are to walk about your gardens, and gather the strawberries ourselves, and sit under trees;—and whatever else you may like to provide, it is to be all out of doors—a table spread in the shade, you know. Everything as natural and simple as possible. Is not that your idea?"
>
> "Not quite. My idea of the simple and the natural will be to have the table spread in the dining-room. The nature and the simplicity of gentlemen and ladies, with their servants and furniture, I think is best observed by meals within doors. When you are tired of eating strawberries in the garden, there shall be cold meat in the house."

Mrs. Elton's idea of a "gipsy party" is given added irony when we consider that the real gipsy party in the novel comes close to attacking Harriet for her money. Yet Mr. Knightley is not simply the spokesman for Jane Austen in his comment. As his name suggests, Mr. Knightley is a slightly anachronistic figure, and his equating "servants" with "furniture" reveals this. His world is a stable, pastoral world in which everything is in its place, people have the predictable stability of furniture, and the virtuous person is always deferred to. This is not the world of Highbury, where gentlewomen sometimes slip to the near-servant status of governess or even, like Miss Bates, to a barely genteel poverty; where governesses become the mistresses of estates; where inhumane behavior surfaces in its members; and, above all, where an encounter of opposites like that between Mr. Knightley and Mrs. Elton can take place.

Highbury is kept on through an endless dialectic. Like a well-oiled machine, it runs on the cooperation and coordination of its parts. Lionel Trilling has come closest to recognizing the basis of cooperation of Highbury, but as I have already suggested, he is mistaken in calling it pastoral. His argument brilliantly articulates a modern bias, for many readers, particularly American readers, view Jane Austen in this way. Cooperation itself is viewed as an archaic phenomenon. But to Jane Austen cooperation was no more pastoral than the moral restrictions in the novels were mysterious taboos. As Trilling states, the pastoral idyll excludes the idea of activity and includes an idea of harmonic stasis. Yet Highbury is an imperfect, changing society. It functions smoothly because almost everyone makes a constant effort to maintain it: "Some change of countenance was necessary for each gentleman as they walked into Mrs. Weston's drawing-room;—Mr. Elton must compose his joyous looks, and Mr. John Knightley disperse his ill-humour. Mr. Elton must smile less, and Mr. John Knightley more, to fit them for the place." These accommodations are minor compared to the continual exertion required of almost all to abide the slowness of Mr. Woodhouse and the loquacity of Miss Bates. I cannot agree with Trilling that everyone except Emma, the "modern" personality, experiences only their charm and goodness. Mr. Knightley must strain to be heard by both, and Jane Fairfax's despair is haunting: "Oh! . . . the comfort of being sometimes alone!" Mr. Woodhouse and Miss Bates are both loved *and* tolerated. Similarly, Mr. Knightley's willingness to move to Hartfield does not assume a lack of will. He is the hero of *Emma* because his move *is* a sacrifice.

Highbury, like all the communities in Jane Austen, is conceived as possessing an almost personal identity and will. "Frank Churchill was looked on as sufficiently belonging to the place to make his merit and prospects a kind of common concern." "By birth [Jane Fairfax] belonged to Highbury." Like Meryton in *Pride and Prejudice*, Highbury ingests and rejects materials that come into it; be it John Knightley's sullenness or Emma's energy, that trait is reworked in such a manner that when it reappears as part of the social body it has been molded to fit a larger purpose. It has become part of the network of influences that, through checks and balances, ensure Highbury's survival. In *Emma*, this process does not reduce the human spirit but expands it; the efforts required of all its members make them better people. The atmosphere of "intelligent love"—when it dominates—is well earned. Many of the dialogues seem to pull and stretch under the strain of accommodation: Emma's little disagreements with her father, Mr. Knightley's conversation with Miss Bates, even Mr. Weston's exchange with Mrs. Elton about his son. At moments the intelligent and sensitive person is forced into irony, and this irony is not a form of social detachment but a form of social adjustment. It is not like the superior sarcasm of Mr. Palmer in *Sense and Sensibility*, which is treated with astringent disapproval. When used sincerely, irony is a benevolent compromise: a way of maintaining social integrity without sacrificing personal integrity, as Emma's first conversation with Mrs. Elton reveals. Such irony is, on the simplest level, courtesy; it is also a method of comprehending reality. In a world where, for reasons beyond the control of the intelligence of the characters, "seldom . . . does complete truth belong to any human disclosure," irony is a more truthful and humble mode of comprehension than direct statement.

Many critics have pointed out that no one works in *Emma*. Yet everyone is working, morally and psychically, to sustain this cooperative enterprise of civilized living. As in *Mansfield Park*, a certain amount of sheer psychic energy is required to make the social order endure. This is difficult for us to fathom, for the modern reader inevitably looks upon inactivity as stagnation; Milton's Adam and Eve in the Garden of Eden before their fall seem to us like old-age pensioners. In *Emma*, those who contribute relatively little to the cooperative enterprise, John Knightley and Jane Fairfax, are either involved or preparing to be involved in the working world. John Knightley has always seemed to me a curiously modern type, a commuting professional man who divides his time entirely between work and family. He and Jane Fairfax lack the energy for Highbury, and through them Austen registers the effect that the breakup of a ruling, or leisure, class will have on refined and civilized values. Austen knew that a community like Highbury could be maintained only if its members took a constant, unflagging interest in one another's welfare. Emma herself instinctively acknowledges this when, upon noticing that Jane Fairfax is not very curious about the news of Mr. Elton's marriage, she remarks, "You are silent, Miss Fairfax—but I hope you mean to take an interest in this news." Like much of Austen's dialogue, even the most offhand comments join in the underlying continuity of the work.

Marriage in *Emma* signifies the validation, not the resolution, of the different dialectics. Frank Churchill's character, Mr. Knightley asserts, "will improve" after his marriage. And as Emma and Mr. Knightley continue to retain their separate identities, we anticipate that cooperation and compromise will maintain the relationship. Emma has had three enlightenments, and we expect that she will experience more.

Mr. Knightley sets the pattern of compromise by moving to Hartfield, an action antithetical to modern ideas of marriage. Yet since the most serious sin in the novel is Emma's insistence that Harriet cut the Martins in order to preserve her own friendship, it follows that

Mr. Knightley should not commit a similar unkindness in making Emma give up her father for him. Since he has no really important relationship to give up in leaving his estate, the sacrifice is proper. Perhaps more significantly, Mr. Knightley's move to Hartfield marks the first time in a Jane Austen novel in which the relationship begins to take precedence over the "place" or estate. Could we imagine Darcy moving to Longbourn? It is also a subtly feminist praise of Mr. Knightley, whose practical sensibility does not include the traditional masculine insistence that his future wife leave her family to become Mrs. Knightley, the mistress of Donwell.

Jane Austen was interested in the stability of form, in what kept the great basic plans of social organization, one of which is marriage, so steadfast throughout whole epochs. To say that this concern is outdated —as several of Austen's critics have reluctantly concluded—reveals a curious misconception. Most people marry, and almost everyone participates in some way in the larger institutions of our society. Yet it has been the preoccupation of a post-Darwinian age to see struggle as the natural state of things and therefore to judge a novelist who explores the implications of our cooperative history as somehow blind or narrow or even trivial.

Why, one may ask, in a novel about social cooperation, is an individual, and a willful individual at that, so undeniably the main subject? Why is the novel not called *Highbury*? The novel as written could not be called *Highbury*; it is clearly a tribute to this heroine whom the author mistakenly thought "no one but myself will much like." Emma even threatens to take control over the work and write her own novel about Harriet: to give her a family history, a personality, beauty and stature, a love affair, a husband, and a social position. This deference to Emma, to her creative impulse, registers the author's interest in the individual person, for whom, after all, society was organized to begin with. Those who forget this origin by placing an abstract social ambition above it—General Tilney, Mrs. Ferrars, Lady Catherine de Bourgh, Sir Walter Elliot—are never contemplated without disapproval. Emma reminds us of what Highbury is for; while she has not the right to remain aloof from it, she has the right to be dissatisfied with it.

Emma is based on a recognition of the life of the individual as a functioning whole that must be coordinated internally before it can function externally. Those who do not coordinate internally—more simply, those, like Harriet, who never know themselves—become the willing victims of those exterior forces that, because they never see them, will always control them. When Arnold Kettle says that the sensitive values of *Emma* are available to one in twenty, he is being generous. They are available to even fewer than that, not even to Emma until the end of the novel. They are available mainly to the intelligent, and only partially to the less intelligent. One does not have to be intelligent to be good in Jane Austen, but one does have to be intelligent to be free, to see and evaluate one's choices. Partly for this reason, an Austen novel seems inexorable beside most Dickens novels. Often in Dickens, in order to be good—above all to be a good woman—one has to be simple-minded. Jane Austen makes us acknowledge the undemocratic truth that those who are born unintelligent are at a terrible disadvantage in the world. Her belief in the importance of education, one of her most constant and serious concerns, is an extension of this awareness.

This is all the more reason why in *Emma* Jane Austen insists on the necessity and finally the benevolence of social cooperation: because it alone protects the Harriets and the Miss Bateses of the world, cares for, tolerates, and loves them. "She must laugh at such a close! Such an end of the doleful disappointments of five weeks back! Such a heart!—such a Harriet!" *Emma* is a novel of human interdependence in every sense. It is Harriet who makes Emma accomplished, Mr. Knightley who makes her witty, Jane Fairfax who makes her average, and, in the closing lines, Mrs. Elton who makes her tasteful:

> The wedding was very much like other weddings, where the parties have no taste for finery or parade; and Mrs. Elton, from the particulars detailed by her husband, thought it all extremely shabby, and very inferior to her own.—"Very little white satin, very few lace veils; a most pitiful business!—Selina would stare when she heard of it."—But, in spite of these deficiencies, the wishes, the hopes, the confidence, the predictions of the small band of true friends who witnessed the ceremony, were fully answered in the perfect happiness of the union.

"In spite of these deficiencies" may be read "because of these deficiencies." In a world that indiscriminately blesses the marriages of Mr. and Mrs. Elton and Harriet and Robert Martin, the union between Emma and Mr. Knightley is surely one of "perfect happiness." We understand them through comparison.

Emma and the Charms of Imagination

Susan Morgan

A man, to be greatly good, must imagine intensely and comprehensively.
—SHELLEY
[and, Mary might have added, a woman must too]

A reading of Jane Austen's fiction may properly begin with the novel whose heroine would think it most natural to be first. Emma Woodhouse, "handsome, clever, and rich," dominates her story with an energy and confidence which distinguishes her from the other heroines of Austen's fiction. Elizabeth Bennet, it is true, also thinks extremely well of herself. But Elizabeth does not have those external supports of beauty, money, and a comfortable home to express her sense of superiority. Her sister is handsomer, and many are richer. Emma, more completely than Elizabeth, seems "to unite some of the best blessings of existence." Emma's joy in being "so always first and always right," as if those two conditions were the same, displays her belief in a direct correspondence between her qualities and her position, her confidence that she merits those blessings of existence. As she so memorably informs Mr. Knightley at the end of the story, "I always deserve the best treatment, because I never put up with any other."

In the course of the novel, Emma, like Captain Wentworth in *Persuasion*, will learn to brook being happier than she deserves. But what does this mean? Of what does her education consist? From Emma's own words, we know that the novel can hardly be read as a lesson in humility.

Emma does not learn that she deserves less than the best treatment. Perhaps, however, she learns that the best treatment is not a matter of deserts, that in her high self-valuation she had not given value enough to the world outside herself. And the moral of the story is not that Emma should think less of herself but that she should value the world more.

Emma's joy in being first is part of what makes her such an exhilarating character. What she offers us, from the beginning to the end, is the conviction that what she thinks about is interesting and valuable. What she offers is a confidence that borders on sublimity in the powers of her own mind. *Emma*, then, is an appropriate starting place for examining Austen's ideas of perception because Emma is Austen's grandest version of a commitment to personal vision. Moreover, Emma's exaltation of her mind's power makes her the very heroine with which to take up the traditional charge that Austen's fiction treats those areas of human experience accessible to reason rather than to feeling and imagination.

The belief that Austen is a novelist of sense implies, in C. S. Lewis's words, that "In her we still breathe the air of the *Rambler* and *Idler*," and she is thus out of place in an age that produced the "Intimations" ode. But more is implied here than historical judgment. Sense, we are to believe, somehow throttles sensibility. This blends with the view that Austen's novels are limited because they are confined to the social and domestic world, the world of drawing rooms and manners and female affairs. Where are the great events, heroic actions, the profound feelings? Where is the French revolution or "Manfred"? A criticism of the class structure? Kurtz's "the horror"? *War and Peace*? Where, in a recent version of Austen's shortcomings, are "the non-human realities which separated from man give him definition and connected give him grandeur"? I know of no other major English novelist about whom critics have been so attentively ingenious in qualifying their appreciations.

The fascination of such charges lies neither in their validity nor in their disavowal of how women marry as a subject for the best fiction, but in the implied assumption that Austen's technical control suggests somehow the limits of her creativity. Probably the finest and most famous expression of this view is Charlotte Brontë's. For her, Austen's novels do not "throb" because they have "confined houses," "a carefully fenced, highly cultivated garden with neat borders," "no open country, no fresh air," and a "Chinese fidelity" in delineating the surface." If one grants that Brontë's allusion to nature is metaphoric as well as a literal claim for the heath and Penistone Crag as the passionate seat of life and art, then what she criticizes is a killing control in Austen's work. Clearly, this criticism has not faded and is central to the problem of Austen's historical place. Brontë's accusation that "the Passions are perfectly unknown to her" echoes again and again: in Lewis's admiring discussions of Austen's moral clarity, her wit, irony, and accurate portrayal of her society; in Angus Wilson's belief that what Austen inherited from Richardson was his "brilliant Grandisonian care for minutiae and mistrust of worldliness; while foreigners preferred Clarissa, Lovelace and passion."

Whether what Marvin Mudrick calls "the literary model of passion" and George Moore called "the burning human heart in English prose narrative" beats in a Clarissa Harlowe or a Marianne Dashwood betrayed by her author, the character in Austen's work most open to the charge of coldness is Emma. Emma herself announces that "I never have been in love; it is not my way, or my nature." Emma discovers that she is mistaken. But even when Mr. Knightley declares himself, the love scene is passed over with the notoriously succinct remark: "What did she say?—Just what she ought, of course. A lady always does." This is a long way from Emily Brontë's *Wuthering Heights*, when Catherine Linton, standing in her nightgown, pale and dying, flings open the window of that stifling bedroom at the Grange to smell the heather on the moor and catch a glimpse of Penistone Crag. Nonetheless, Emma Woodhouse is one of the great characters in the English novel. As Trilling has said, Emma is one of those rare heroines with a moral life of her own. And that moral life means learning the proper relation of imagination to truth. Far from being of limited significance, this is more than equal to great loves or great wars as a subject for fiction. Austen need not provide scenes of passionate intimacy as well.

Yet we do need to consider what emotion means in *Emma*. Emma offers her own view in a revery on tenderness, as a way of rationalizing her unjust preference for Harriet Smith over Jane Fairfax. Harriet has just declared her gratitude to Emma because, as Harriet so appealingly puts it, "Nobody is equal to you!—I care for nobody as I do for you!"

> "There is no charm equal to tenderness of heart," said she afterwards to herself. "There is nothing to be compared to it. Warmth and tenderness of heart, with an affectionate, open manner, will beat all the clearness of head in the world, for attraction. I am sure it will. It is tenderness of heart which makes my dear father so generally beloved—which gives Isabella all her popularity."

The effect of the quotation is to remind us that we are inside a person's consciousness. And what we see in Emma's revery is its disguised selfishness. Emma is not concerned with real warmth and is probably proud of her supposed lack of tenderness, because she sees tenderness as a negative attribute. To her it means weakness, lack of will, a softness of character which allows itself to be controlled, a softness which Harriet has and Jane Fairfax does not. Emma generously grants tenderness to Isabella and Mr. Woodhouse as well as to Harriet, three characters alike in their sweetness and fluttering concern for others. That may be fine for them, but not for Emma Woodhouse. Such tenderness means surrender of self. To Emma, never loath to be first, it means not being first. Emma is right. We would not like to see her exhibit such symptoms of a full heart as dear Harriet's cotton-lined box of "Most Precious Treasures," Isabella's missionary zeal on the subject of gruel, and Mr. Woodhouse's kindly attempts to protect those about him from fresh air. For these simple characters being tender is being weak and silly. Even a cold heart seems preferable.

Yet the most loving hearts in this book belong to the strong—to Robert Martin, John and George Knightley, Jane Fairfax, and, at the last, to Emma. Children, it is said, think all the world is part of them. So does Emma. Like the emperor of Lilliput, Emma has a dominion which stretches to the very extremities of the globe and includes all Highbury. And it is just as fictional. Emma Woodhouse, "handsome, clever, and rich," at twenty years of age is still a child. In that childishness Emma resembles her father, who is "never able to suppose that other people could feel differently from himself." Within her small world she knows no boundaries, recognizes no limits. And because there is no point for Emma where her sphere of influence ends, there is no room for anyone else's to begin. For Emma, growing up is learning the limits of self: as her domain shrinks the real world enlarges. Emma learns that people have an internal life of their own and that the recognition of this personal existence, this self in someone else, is the necessary requisite for morality and for love.

As Emma stands at the doorway of Ford's, waiting for Harriet to choose a muslin, she looks with complacency at the quiet street scene and muses that "A mind lively and at ease, can do with seeing nothing, and can see nothing that does not answer." Emma's smugness doesn't surprise us. She had used the same tone in assuring Harriet that she had no need of ever marrying, since "If I know myself, Harriet, mine is an active, busy mind." Emma will see what she wants even if it is not there, and will not see what she doesn't want even if it is. Her responsibility and her manipulations are emphasized in that Austen never allows her to be wrong from ignorance. Both Knightley's, for example, warn her of Mr. Elton. She is explicitly shown the truth and she insists on her conceptions in spite of it. Emma's fancies, her manipulations, her imagination, are all those of a creator. She makes it up and thinks it's real, not allowing the truth to violate her creation.

Emma creates from love of power and love of self, but also because she believes that without her imagination acting upon it, the world would be a bore. But it is Austen, and not Emma Woodhouse, who imagines this world and gives life to other characters besides Emma. As Tave remarks, "a better imagination has been creating a wiser structure." Emma's fault is not that she sees herself as a perceptive observer but that she considers herself a creator and the people around her as expressions of her will. Emma is a matchmaker because she believes that people will feel as she wishes. Yet even grateful Harriet, who had given herself over to be formed, surprises Emma by having a feeling of her own.

For most of the story Emma is incapable of seeing or understanding other people except in relation to her own concerns. She cannot, in imagination, put herself in someone else's place, because she has yet to imagine that others have a place. Her attitude is seen in her response to Harriet's question of whether she has ever noticed Mr. Martin:

> "A young farmer, whether on horseback or on foot, is the very last sort of person to raise my curiosity. The yeomanry are precisely the order of people with whom I feel I can have nothing to do. A degree or two lower, and a creditable appearance might interest me; I might hope to be useful to their families in some way or other. But a farmer can need none of my help, and is therefore in one sense as much above my notice as in every other he is below it."

In remarks like these Emma's superior attitude to her environment approaches the divine.

Emma's inability to see or care for people except in the terms she sets for them makes her unaware that others have their own self-conceptions, even their own hopes and plans. Thus, with all her snobbish sensitivity to her own social position, she can't see far enough to recognize Mr. Elton's sense of his. If she cares so much for place, why should she think he wouldn't? Probably because she doesn't think of him at all. She has no grasp of his situation and aspirations, not even in the face of Mr. Knightley's explicit warning. That is easily dismissed "when she considered that Mr. Knightley could not have observed him as she had done, neither with the interest, nor (she must be allowed to tell herself, in spite of Mr. Knightley's pretensions) with the skill of such an observer on such a question as herself." Mr. Knightley, it is true, has not the benefit of seeing through her eyes.

In spite of Emma's ability to ignore facts, no one will actually live in her make-believe world. Mr. Elton's proposal is her first surprise, and it is a gross and terrible scene for her. Mr. Elton is certainly a repulsive lover. But we are in a comedy, and neither the proposal nor Emma's sense of insult are very significant. The power of the scene and its horror for her come, I think, from the pain resulting when truth so literally violates imagination. Emma cannot very well pretend that Mr. Elton has not rapturously seized her hand. Because she is so obviously wrong, because she must relinquish her scheme, her dominion is diminished. She does, indeed, lose a part of herself when Mr. Elton asserts his existence outside her mind. Emma does not learn from this scene. It is only the beginning.

Emma always loves herself because she lives in her mind and it seems the world to her. She doesn't realize that others may also live in theirs. Her strange ignorance about her love for Mr. Knightley surely comes from that childish lack of discrimination in which all feelings are part of loving oneself. Not until she has to realize that Mr. Knightley can live in ways separate to his relation to her, ways that she would be excluded from, does she see his independence. Learning that Harriet has her own ideas for him, Emma is shocked into self-knowledge. "It darted through her, with the speed of an arrow, that Mr. Knightley must marry no one but herself!" When Emma was a little girl Mr. Knightley, like all adults, had been part of her domain (though he was distinctive in his critical view of her). But Emma grows up. She prompts Mr. Knightley's declaration and her own happiness by that new-learned consciousness which allows her to put his feelings ahead of her own. "Emma could not bear to give him pain. He was wishing to confide in her—perhaps to consult her;—cost her what it would, she would listen." This is a classic scene in Austen's fiction. We see Emma's moral imagination at its best, in her selfless and generous sympathy for Mr. Knightley's point of view at the very moment she is filled with misery for her own. It is Emma's most imaginative act. Through it, we know she loves him and deserves him.

Mr. Knightley, it is true, also succumbs to the fault of judging another through the distorting perspective of his own interests. He is jealous. And hearing of Frank's engagement to Jane, he goes to comfort Emma, the "sweetest and best of all creatures, faultless in spite of all her faults." "He had found her agitated and low. — Frank Churchill was a villain. — He heard her declare that she had never loved him. Frank Churchill's character was not desperate. — She was his own Emma, by hand and word, when they returned into the house; and if he could have thought of Frank Churchill then, he might have deemed him a very good sort of fellow." But apart from this endearing exception, Mr. Knightley is the one person who does consistently grant other people a personal existence.

Mr. Knightley is probably not more intelligent than Emma. Yet he often sees the true attitudes and situations of other people because he has acknowledged their internal lives apart from his wishes or plans. He is not just older than Emma, he has grown up. He recognizes social and material ambition in Mr. Elton and can think to send the carriage for Jane Fairfax because he sympathizes with her plight. His kindness to Miss Bates consists precisely in insisting on her right to recognition; on the dignity of being a separate person whose feelings must be taken into account. Miss Bates does not exist in order that Emma can make up a card table for her father. Mr. Knightley forces Emma to look at Miss Bates as a person rather than as a means, inconsequential in herself, of Emma's entertainment; to see her situation, to acknowledge that she has feelings which Emma has seriously hurt. It is a sad truth for the girl never loath to be first, but regardless of Emma, people will go about thinking their own thoughts, having their own emotions, and living their own lives. Even Miss Bates, however sunk in fortune, has a kingdom of her own.

In terms of fictional conventions we would most expect Jane Fairfax to be the heroine of *Emma*. We know, on the unimpeachable authority of Emma's jealousy, that Jane is elegant, accomplished, intelligent, and beautiful. Her charm is marred only by a reserve which turns out to be more than excusable because of the secret with which she has suffered. Jane comes from the external world, the big world of real events, to the idyllic isolation of Highbury. Because she brings the disturbing facts of life into a hitherto tranquil realm easily governed by Emma's imagination, Jane is a threat to Emma, although not as the rival Emma envisions. Jane is poor. She arrives in Highbury with pressing burdens, conflicts, and feelings. Her situation is such that her decisions and acts, and those of others unaware of her situation, will have lifelong consequences for her. Unlike anyone else, Jane is introduced in a moment of crisis. Events will soon bring lasting happiness or despair, and she has the superior intelligence and the emotional sensitivity to be aware of her situation.

Such a brilliantly dramatic situation is the stuff of which novels are made. Jane Fairfax, with all the advantages which nature and upbringing can provide, is being forced by circumstances into an inferior existence. Throughout the story Jane suffers her aunt's endless chatter, Mrs. Elton's condescension, and Frank's cruel flirting, suffers until she makes herself ill. And while Jane languishes in her cramped room with her garrulous aunt, Frank gone, and nothing to hope for but the crass fate of looking after other people's children, we are with Emma, sending her "some arrow-root of very superior quality."

Jane Fairfax, so dark, quiet, and apart, has interested many readers. What is this girl who has been given the same name as her author, and who so tantalizingly fits the idea of a real heroine doing in the book? She is Marianne and Elinor Dashwood rolled into one. And yet we see little of her, know little about her. One major reason, after all, is that the novel is Emma's. And Emma is flawed. We cannot be allowed into Jane's mind—or even see too much of her in company—without endangering our sympathy with Emma. Wayne Booth has provided a concise analysis of Jane's position:

> Emma must shine supreme. It is not only that the slightest glance inside Jane's mind would be fatal to all of the author's plans for mystification about Frank Churchill, though this is important. The major problem is that any extended view of her would reveal her as a more sympathetic person than Emma herself. Jane is superior to Emma in most respects except the stroke of good fortune that made Emma the heroine of the book. In matters of taste and ability, of head and of heart, she is Emma's superior, and Jane Austen, always in danger of losing our sympathy for Emma, cannot risk any degree of distraction.

Jane, then, must stay unknown. But why has that "stroke of good fortune" been Emma's, why is the novel about her? Why, since she is more deserving, isn't it about Jane? And what is the significance of its not being about her?

One's sense of Jane is always that she is outside, partly because Jane does not truly belong to Highbury (she enters the story late), partly because Emma does not befriend her as she should, but primarily because Jane has an independent sense of herself. She has, in Emma's words, "such apparent indifference whether she pleased or not." Emma does not meet people halfway. Rather, she absorbs them into her world. This happens both imaginatively and literally. Mr. Knightley customarily takes the initiative by walking over to pay a visit, and Emma simply sends the carriage for whatever other society she wants. When befriended, Harriet comes to Hartfield for long visits, and the manipulation of Mr. Elton's heart mainly occurs there. The parties at Donwell Abbey and Box Hill are exceptions, and at these events Emma is significantly out of control. But generally the focus is Hartfield, where Emma can receive visitors with the secure sense of absolute dominion.

The comic aspect of Emma's self-centeredness is represented by her father, whose "neighbours knew that he loved to be inquired after." Yet Emma herself has too much life to be satisfied with ruling Hartfield, and her increasing connection with other people can be gauged by the number of late scenes which do indeed take her away from home. The Cole party is a good example. Emma wouldn't think of going. Yet her snobbery is countered by the fact that initially she is not invited, and finally it is overcome by the thought that her friends—and Frank Churchill—will be there. The chance for liveliness, for fun, attracts her in spite of herself. "Might not the evening end in a dance? had been a question of his. The bare possibility of it acted as a further irritation on her spirits; and her being left in solitary grandeur, even supposing the omission to be intended as a compliment, was but poor comfort." Of course, Emma goes, because she cannot bear to be left out. And that is the problem. Her desire to be first restricts Emma to the limited relations where she can so be and conflicts with her desire to be at the center of Highbury affairs.

Emma's failed relations to other people are immediately established as a problem. The novel opens with Emma's loss of Miss Taylor, her fear of "intellectual solitude," and need for a new companion and friend. Emma chooses Harriet Smith, who will bring dullness rather than excitement and thus sustain the very isolation Emma needs to overcome. Harriet, in Emma's view of her, is a heroine from sentimental fiction: fair, sweet, and seventeen, with "those soft blue eyes and all those natural graces" and an unexplained past. Like many an author or a hero of such novels, Emma decides to give that natural beauty the improvement of a little art. But true to the convention, Harriet is both shallow and predictable, and Austen mocks the sensitivity of such sentimental creations in scenes such as Harriet trying to choose a ribbon at Ford's or surrendering her precious mementos of Mr. Elton: the piece of court plaster he didn't use or the pencil lacking lead.

Emma's attempt to shape Harriet is presented as immoral both because Emma chooses power over real friendship and because she takes advantage of Harriet's "weak head" to violate Harriet's own tastes and inclinations. As Austen had shown in the relations between Henry and Eleanor Tilney and Catherine Morland, proper influence honors the integrity of self. Emma's counseling Harriet to refuse Mr. Martin because she has just begun the business of getting a husband and should not throw herself away on the first offer looks forward to another instance of false persuasion, when for similar reasons Lady Russell convinces Anne Elliot to break her engagement to Captain Wentworth. Both of these young women end by marrying the man they had been counseled against. But Anne has not the foolishness of Harriet, and Lady Russell, for all her snobbishness, has not the vanity of Emma.

The friend Emma should have chosen is Jane, the only character close to her in age, accomplishments, and consciousness—in many ways Emma's superior. That is why Emma, who prefers power to equality, does not befriend Jane. When Emma relents and sends the arrowroot, Jane will have nothing to do with her. Refusing to go outside herself and grant the independence of other people must finally cost Emma something tangible. It costs her Jane. If Harriet is fair and sentimental, Jane is the dark, realistic heroine whose history most fulfills Emma's fancies: by not knowing her, Emma misses the romantic intrigue that's actually occurring. That she need not have is clear from Frank's belief that she knew. Fiddling with romances for Harriet, Emma missed the one that truly burned.

Throughout the story Jane is presented as the mystery person in Highbury, not only for Emma but also for the other characters and the reader. She arouses a curiosity not explained by our simply wanting to know her secret: we know about the engagement after one reading, and yet the curiosity is still there, still unsatisfied. The clues which ostensibly point to the secret of the engagement actually work to make us want to become better acquainted with Jane. Thus, in the Hartfield dinner discussion of her walk to the post office in the rain, there can be no doubt about what she is concealing: she has had a letter from Frank. And by the end of the dinner, when Mr. Weston announces that Frank is returning to Highbury, we know its contents. But the real interest of the scene lies not in the bald fact of her receiving a letter (an event which, we know from *Sense and Sensibility*, should presuppose an engagement), but in wondering how Jane feels about it, what it means to her. What she does say has a sadness which seems inappropriate after learning that Frank will soon be back. Clearly, we are not to be allowed to attribute typical or predictable sensations to her. And when we would hear more from Jane, she is "deep in conversation with John Knightley" and not to be interrupted.

Throughout the story Austen places obstacles between the reader and Jane, the most major, of course, being Emma and Frank. We are often led to expect a privileged view of Jane and Frank's private encounters, and are for the most part disappointed. The epitome of these moments occurs at the Coles' party. Frank contrives to speak to Jane by pretending he will ask her something embarrassing. "Emma soon saw him standing before Miss Fairfax, and talking to her; but as to its effect on the young lady, as he had improvidently placed himself exactly between them, exactly in front of Miss Fairfax, she could absolutely distinguish nothing." The reader, limited to seeing from the same physical perspective as Emma, also distinguishes nothing. The difference is that the reader can imagine that something is going on. And how Jane might react to Frank at that party is an interesting question, and one without an obvious answer.

The other characters share and increase the reader's curiosity about Jane. Frank, Emma, Mrs. Weston, Mr. Cole, Mrs. Elton, and Mr. Knightley—all speculate about her. The conditions of Jane's life are awkward enough; yet even the most observant characters do not know how she feels. Consider how frequently people remark of Jane that they don't understand how she bears her situation. Does she miss the Campbells and Mrs. Dixon? Why does she allow herself to be patronized by Mrs. Elton? How can she live with her aunt? What does she think of Emma's flirting or Frank's sending the pianoforte? That famous reserve simply increases speculation and gives away nothing. We don't know Jane's mind or heart at all.

Finally, the secret engagement is revealed and Jane is free to be candid and unreserved. What happens? Jane leaves in a carriage with Mrs. Weston and opens her heart. But the curious reader isn't allowed to be present and receives only the briefest account. Similarly, the last opportunity for getting acquainted with Jane occurs when a chastened Emma goes to her home to offer apologies, friendship, and intimacy. There sits Mrs. Elton, whose presence effectively destroys any hope of speaking freely with Jane, and the reader's disappointment is as great as

Emma's. The single unreserved moment that Emma, or the reader, is allowed with Jane is that hurried expression of apology and good feeling in the hall—sufficient to be assured of Jane's natural warmth and charm, but not enough to know her. Emma treats Jane badly, but she treats others badly as well, and we do not need the example of Jane to condemn Emma's blind vanity. Jane's special role is to hold out the promise of people of value outside the self, a promise which, in the case of Jane Fairfax, is deliberately unfulfilled.

Jane's presence in the novel adds an important dimension to understanding Emma, one which works to justify Emma's imaginative point of view. When the secret engagement is revealed we emerge from the mind into the arena of events. While Emma toyed with stories about Jane's heart being broken, Jane's heart was being broken, in part by Emma's irresponsible flirting. We learn that there is no escape into imagination. But we learn something even more important. Jane's world, that place outside Emma's control, is not so very dull after all. Exciting and unpredictable things do happen in idyllic Highbury, even in Miss Bates's tiny, drab rooms. Emma's isolating manipulations are wrong not just because they are vain or harmful or untrue, but because they don't provide what she wants. Trilling makes this point beautifully when discussing Emma's wish to form Harriet:

> Yet the destiny is not meanly conceived, the act is meant to be truly creative—she wants Harriet to be distinguished and not a commonplace person, she wants nothing to be common place, she requires of life that it be well-shaped and impressive, and alive. It is out of her insistence that the members of the picnic shall begin being witty and cease being dull that there comes her famous insult to Miss Bates. Her requirement that life be vivid is too often expressed in terms of social deportment—she sometimes talks like a governess or a dowager—but it is, in its essence, a poet's demand.

Emma's vanity is more that of an artist than a god. Perhaps that is why Austen can make Emma's playing at creativity such an attractive sin. A desire to make life vivid is surely possible to forgive.

Emma is a creator whose creations violate the inner lives of the people she tries to control. And Emma learns to recognize the presumptuousness of her manipulations, to accept her limits and the inviolability of others. Yet this educational process should not stifle Emma. Relinquishing imagination is too great a price for clearsightedness. Because knowing Emma has entertained us, we are on her side and accept that she has a right to demand entertainment as well. We want her to be good, and not only because it is right or even because Emma will be rewarded by awaking to her true love for Mr. Knightley. That neither the moral imperative nor the reward is enough is one reason why *Emma* is a great novel, and Austen the first great modern novelist.

Why should Emma be good? Why should she know the truth? Truth, in this novel, is that individuals have an inner life apart from other people's wishes for them, an inner life that cannot immediately be experienced by someone else but must be honored nonetheless. Growing up is learning that the self does not encompass the entire world. It is a sort of shrinking into definable shape. But why grow up? The novel is about, for one thing, the inviolability of the self; the inviolability of Harriet Smith, Miss Bates, and even Mr. Elton. This applies as much to the author's relation to Emma as it does to Emma's relations to the other characters. She must not be betrayed, even in the name of truth.

Reality, or the truth Emma comes to know, is not in conflict with imagination. On the contrary, knowing one's own limits is the precondition for imagination. For imagination presumes an ignorance which Emma initially would not accept. Simply put, if no one can see directly into someone else, then knowing another has to be an imaginative act. In *Emma* this creativity is both moral and emotional, since an imaginative leap toward knowing another is, by definition, sympathetic. That is why the most loving hearts in the book belong to the strong people. Tenderness means the sympathetic perception of the independent existence of other human beings. Yet Emma's liveliness is so valuable that if "facing reality" were to deprive her of it she would be better to turn away. It is Emma's brilliant vitality, her supreme good health, her energy of mind and heart, which gives her moral stature. If she is to accept her limits and actively put her attentiveness and her interest in people outside her control, we need an assurance that the trust is not misplaced. Truth may be its own end, but to win Emma it needs the added luster of being able to realize the hopes of imagination.

Emma is not a book about mature understanding replacing immature fancy. Nor is it about a girl's fear of involvement in life being overcome. It is about the powers of the individual mind, the powers of sympathy and imagination, and about how these powers can find their proper objects in the world outside the mind. The heroine insists that life be interesting and tries to make it so. She makes the child's demand that she be entertained. But the source of that demand is her imagination. Emma's demand is valid; the largeness of her claims on life gives her greatness, in spite of her faults. The claim of the novel is that life is interesting, that fact can be as delightful as fiction, that imagination need not be in conflict with reality.

At the end of the novel Emma marries Mr. Knightley and is assured of happiness. For Mr. Knightley, who sees her lovingly and clearly, she is "faultless in spite of all her faults." But Emma can no longer think of herself as first because there is someone else in the world. And that someone else is not Mr. Knightley. It is Jane Fairfax. Jane must leave Highbury without ever satisfying that wish to know her which the author has so deliberately created. *Emma* celebrates the joys of close family connections, well-known scenes, "very old friends." It is a story in which the ideal of a lover has turned out to be a relative and neighbor since childhood, in which the idyll of perfect happiness is to be lived without leaving home. But Highbury is not a closed world. And Jane is our promise that there are interesting people yet to become acquainted with. Austen can send her heroine out from the proven delights of her own mind into the world of other people because she has provided someone worth making that journey for.

What Emma learns by the end of the story has been present for the reader throughout in the narrative technique. The leap which takes writer and reader into the minds of characters is impossible in life but common in novels. Austen is the first writer in English fiction to make this privileged perspective a major technique. She uses "free indirect speech" to see into a character and to see from that character's point of view. Certainly, as Booth has pointed out, seeing into Emma provides sympathy for her as well as knowledge of her faults:

> By showing most of the story through Emma's eyes, the author insures that we will travel with Emma rather than stand against her. . . . the sustained inner view leads the reader to hope for good fortune for the character with whom he travels, quite independently of the qualities revealed.

This inside view has become necessary because of Austen's sense of the difficulties of perception, her conviction that there is a space between an inner and outer view. What people or characters in books say and do is not enough to know them by. There are, of course, acts that by themselves condemn the doers. But villains are rare and easily judged. Austen concerns herself with the more difficult and more subtle problem of how to understand those around us and ourselves. Morality in *Emma*, as in all Austen's novels, is not a code, or norm, or principle, which one can live and die by. Instead, it is a way of seeing which includes within its definition some sort of candor or affection. Judgment is seldom conclusive, never infallible. So we understand best and judge best when aided by sympathy and imagination. Austen lets us understand Emma by allowing us, for a little while, to live in her mind.

Austen called Emma a character "whom no one but myself will much like," but it is clear that the joy and pleasure of the book depend upon caring about Emma. Certainly, the external events are not gripping. There are no abductions or seductions, no rapes or near rapes, no murders or stray babies, no stirring adventures, no dark deeds, no characters beneath contempt or even above reproach. There are a few gypsies who wander in and scare Harriet, but they seem a little silly in the environs of Highbury and are soon dispatched. In fact, they remind us that it is not Harriet's rescue from them but her rescue on the dance floor which actually matters. Not only does nothing out of the way happen—very little happens at all. There are some dinners, a couple of parties, one secret engagement, and even a few marriages. We do learn by hearsay of trips, a death, and a birth. In *Emma* the lack of large-scale events is a prominent fact. This is characteristic of Austen. Nonetheless, *Emma* is an extreme case. Less happens in this novel than in any of her others. It is the only one set all in one place, and Emma the only heroine who is never away from home.

Emma is also extreme in the decency of its characters. Austen was never directly interested in villains, but in all her other novels there is at least one man and one woman who are wicked. We do hear about Mrs. Churchill, and the Eltons are both crude and cruel. But they do not compare, at least in their actions, to Isabella Thorpe and General Tilney, Wickham and Lady Catherine de Bourgh, Willoughby and Lucy Steele, Henry Crawford and Mrs. Norris, or Mr. Elliot and Mrs. Clay. Some of these people do horrible things. The Eltons are probably capable of meanness beyond their public cruelty to Harriet or their excruciating officiousness to Jane Fairfax. And Mrs. Churchill could have swooped down like Lady Catherine if Austen had wished to advance her story by external conflict, by having the not-so-nice people get in the way of the nice. But Highbury is an idyll, and its evil characters are ineffectual.

The only character whose actions provide obstacles to the deserved happiness of others is Emma herself. Her snobbery damages Robert Martin as Lady Catherine had tried to damage Elizabeth Bennet, and she flirts as self-indulgently as Mary Crawford. We side with Elizabeth and Fanny, and with farmer Martin and Jane. Still, by what Booth calls that "stroke of good fortune," Emma is the heroine. We don't turn a page to see Robert Martin get his girl or even to see Mr. Knightley get his, but just to see more of Emma.

Emma's power to interest the reader is inseparable from her power to interest herself. Emma will always love herself. In thinking of what she learns it is clear that the aim is not to relinquish her self-love. It is almost the end of the story when Emma makes that wonderful remark to Mr. Knightley that "I always deserve the best treatment, because I never put up with any other." Emma's love of herself is part of what makes her creative and part of why she asks so much of her world. Trilling, writing of Emma's appeal, observes:

> We cannot be slow to see what is the basis of this energy and style and intelligence. It is self-love. There is a great power of charm in self-love, although, to be sure, the charm is an ambiguous one. We resent it and resist it, yet we are drawn by it, if only it goes with a little grace or creative power. Nothing is easier to pardon than the mistakes and excesses of self-love: if we are quick to condemn them, we take pleasure in forgiving them. And with good reason, for they are the extravagance of the first of virtues, the most basic and biological of the virtues, that of self preservation. . . . We understand self-love to be part of the moral life of all men; in men of genius we expect it to appear in unusual intensity and we take it to be an essential element of their power. The extraordinary thing about Emma is that she has a moral life as a man has a moral life.

In *Emma* loving oneself is the necessary condition for morality and imagination. This had already been true for heroes. Austen has transformed the idea of the heroine in English fiction by making it true of Emma.

When Mr. Knightley tells her that Robert Martin has at last got Harriet, Emma is relieved and grateful that her interference had in the end not been irretrievable. She vows humility and circumspection: "Serious she was, very serious in her thankfulness, and in her resolutions; and yet there was no preventing a laugh, sometimes in the very midst of them." Without that laugh Emma's joy in her world would have shrunk. For Harriet's fluctuating heart is comical. Emma is not too reformed to appreciate that. Early in the novel, after the pain of telling Harriet Mr. Elton's true intentions, Emma had made a similar resolution, of "being humble and discreet, and repressing imagination all the rest of her life." But Emma has done no such thing. For imagination, like tenderness, belongs to the strong people. To repress it would be to repress the power of the self to reach out and make significant "all those little matters on which the daily happiness of private life depends."

Emma is about the inviolability of the self, a morality grounded on a sympathetic and imaginative perception of the selves of others, an awareness of the limits of such perception, and a claim for the value rather than just the right of facts to dominate fictions. Some important facts about *Emma* are that it was published in 1816, written after *Mansfield Park*, after *Lyrical Ballads*, after the revolution in France. In other words, Austen wrote *Emma* well into what literary historians call the English romantic period, and it is her next-to-last finished book. She wrote *Emma* when she was thirty-nine, and there is little evidence for believing that she felt very much older or more autumnal four and a half months later when she began *Persuasion*. Moreover, apart from the unresolved question of *Northanger Abbey*, all five novels were either written or revised into the form we know them between 1809 and 1817. Whatever earlier versions there may have been, the versions we have are from Austen's mature Chawton period, all written or revised in the same place within a few years. They share not only time and place. They also share a historical concern about perception and judgment. That concern is central to understanding Austen's work in a way that such questions as whether she was passionate or limited or ironic or conservative or learned romance as she grew older simply are not. It is time to accept that Jane Austen belongs in the romantic age and that her subject is perception as an epistemological as well as a moral question.

While Austen's work was transforming the idea of the English novel, Wordsworth's work was similarly transforming the idea of English poetry. Her novels are no more the harmonious climax of some rational and social tradition than his poetry is a fluttering up into emotional flight. In their respective genres, they are true revolutionaries. These disparate artists sharing a historical moment also share a new attitude to their art, an attitude which includes a commitment to deriving meaning and value from ordinary language, normal people, and everyday life (even though what each meant by these terms differed considerably). Tave, in an important bicentenary essay on Austen and Wordsworth, offers an impressive description of the "points at which they touch." He reminds us that they are, both of them, "poets of marriage," and that they both have "a sense of duty understood and deeply felt by those who see the integrity and peace of their own lives as essentially bound to the lives of others and see the lives of all in a more than merely social order."

Within this sense of a "more than merely social order" there is a special affinity between *Emma* and Wordsworth's "Intimations" ode. Wordsworth is the English poet most associated with the theme of growing up. For him this means moving from subjective unity with the universe toward learning to distinguish and accept the boundaries between oneself and "outward things." The ode, in all its visionary power, describes "the development of a sense of reality." And for Wordsworth as for Austen, boundaries are the condition for morality and for love. In order for the emotions to have an object, the self must be distinguished from others and from the natural world. The ode, in Harold Bloom's words, is "about separateness and consequent mortality, and about the imaginative power that can bridge that separateness and so intimate an immortality that is in turn, just and only, 'primal sympathy' of one human with another." The novel closest in time and in topic to the ode is *Emma*.

Both the ode and *Emma* are centrally concerned with the growth of a person's consciousness, "the philosophic mind." And the choice of subject alone distinguished their authors from their predecessors in English literature. Of course, for Wordsworth the process is dreaded because it is a move from the glories of unconsciousness to a consciousness of one's mortality, a move weighted with the ambivalence of any fortunate fall. Austen's view is more mundane. Imagination and sympathy do not have the stature of immortal intimations. And yet for her, as for Wordsworth, they are the means of vision. Maturity involves an ability to understand which cannot be limited to rational knowledge. Neither reason nor fact will do for understanding Jane Fairfax, or for understanding Emma. Emma moves from a view which subsumes others in her sense of self, to being able to see them as existing independently of her and thus being able to love them.

There are, of course, deep and essential differences between Austen and Wordsworth, but these have always been visible. Their affinities help us to see the centrality of the problem of reaching beyond the self in *Emma* and the characteristic of that problem as more than a matter of individual ethics. The very uniqueness of Emma's character means that a leap beyond the self does not include self-denial or humility or a control which represses feeling and imagination. Our recognition of Emma's power can also lead us to recognize that her story transforms the conventions of the novel of education. The greatness of Emma's conception is that through her Austen explores not only what we are obliged to learn but also what we have a right to hope for in "the best blessings of existence." Events must be equal to character. Anything less than "perfect happiness" for Emma would mean not a just fate but the failure of experience. What Austen offers Emma is a life which fulfills her hopes, "the ordered form and truth of the plot which, from start to finish, meets her at every turn as it maintains its beautiful and inevitable course." The brilliance of Emma's imperfect character matched with the extravagant yet deserved joyousness of that "perfect" fate make *Emma* one of the rare celebratory works of English fiction.

If we ask what Austen celebrates in *Emma* we need to return to the question of Austen's historical place and the charge that she lacks depth of feeling. That charge finally cannot be refuted. Whatever its source, the novel often used to represent passion against Austen's work is Richardson's *Clarissa*. Certainly, *Clarissa* is a novel of powerful feeling and Clarissa herself the first great heroine of English fiction. She is the only heroine of eighteenth-century fiction equal in conception to Emma, and I can think of no other heroine before Emma who is at once as grand and as different. But the differences between these two novels ought not to be described in terms of depth of feeling. Further, most of the differences between *Emma* and *Clarissa* need not be mentioned here. I want to look briefly at *Clarissa* in order to suggest one area of contrast with *Emma* which I hope will point to historical rather than emotional terms for distinguishing them.

Clarissa, in all its emotional and psychological power, can be called a novel of principles. Richardson provides a fixed standard of moral rightness which is presumed throughout the action and is accepted by his characters and by the reader. There is no problem of judgment and so no question of moral growth or of the development of moral consciousness. In spite of Clarissa's difficulty in admitting her attraction to Lovelace and her continual self-deceptions about that attraction, the action of the novel does not consist, even in part, of her movement to self-awareness. That simply is not what the novel is about. Richardson's characters, whether themselves good or evil, do not call into question the criteria of judgment. In fact, the acceptance of these criteria is the prerequisite for the action. Lovelace knows he's wicked and Clarissa knows she's good. And there is no change in their moral positions. That, of course, is what generates much of the plot. Clarissa wants to stay good and reform Lovelace, while Lovelace wants to stay wicked and corrupt Clarissa. Moral fixity is what they are fighting about.

Clarissa's dilemma is that she is inextricably caught in a situation and yet must think and act in accordance with an ideal of behavior and with complete disregard for the situation. She must not take circumstances into account; she must maintain her innocence in the world of experience. Clarissa's romantic counterpart is probably William Blake's Thel, who flees from the ugliness of sex and mortality back to the innocent Vales of Har. But of course, for Blake, Thel's flight is not a return to heaven but a fall into stifling emptiness. There is no creativity without generation. Blake might approve of Austen's vision of Emma, who, unlike Clarissa and Thel, moves successfully out to experience without giving up the creative power of her mind.

Marriage is a union with life, and Austen can conclude *Emma* by giving her heroine the "perfect happiness" of such a union, because Emma has opened herself to the world. Clarissa's progress, on the other hand, is necessarily a withdrawal. Clarissa is a true innocent, and her story is one of innocence sustained. Trusting to her principles she is always guided aright. Her values do not emerge from living in the world, because there are no truths to be learned from particulars or situations. For Richardson human involvement is a secondary good. Clarissa's victory and her glory is precisely that she does not change, that she is not transformed by her fate. A child of her heavenly Father throughout, she has remained essentially unrelated to this life, and ends by entering into his house.

The fundamental conflict between the realms of the ideal and the real is carried to its extreme when Clarissa can disregard the fact that she has literally been raped because in her mind she is still pure. Mere act cannot change her. Richardson's point is not just that value does not grow out of experience. Experience is in direct conflict with the sources of value. And *Clarissa* is appropriately a novel of battle. The relation of the real world to the Christian ideal is one of violation and, on the other side, of salvation.

Richardson, unlike Austen or Wordsworth, sees morality as absolute in the sense that the definition of goodness can't be shaped or transformed by the particulars of character or situation. One consequence is that there are no small sins in the characters in *Clarissa*. Everything in the novel has the quality of being larger than life. Clarissa is a perfect angel and Lovelace a perfect villain. There are few virgins with her tenacity, few seducers with his persistence. This largeness is enhanced by an atmosphere of improbability. There is nothing familiar or mundane about Clarissa's story. It is a tale full of strange characters and strange events. Although it depicts the triumph of the pure in heart, the history of that triumph is one of wildness and woe. Everything about Clarissa—her purity, her propriety, her trials—sets her apart. Yet once the reader accepts the fantastic premises of Clarissa's nature and her situation, her spectacular letters are consistent and appropriate and, in that sense, believably "real."

The difference between *Clarissa* and *Emma* can be best seen by asking if Emma is virtuous—assuming that virtue means something other than simple virginity. The question is clearly inappropriate because we cannot think of Emma in Richardson's terms. *Emma* is cast in a relativistic world. Richardson's moral standards do not apply to Emma because she has a quality which in Richardson's vision does not, and need not, exist: she has imagination. It gives her what Trilling calls "her modern consciousness," letting her come out with the fact that Miss Bates is a bore. Imagination implies that characters and situations differ in ways that matter, and therefore how one ought to think and act will differ too. Moral vision grows out of relations to people and experiences. It is a process, rather than a definable standard asserting general truth.

Austen's concern is with the familiar, the likely, the concrete. Clarissa's moral and emotional stance has a grandeur in the exciting and wicked London of Richardson's novel which is out of place, even a bit silly, in Highbury. We can get some idea of the enormous distance between the two books by recalling that the central immoral act equivalent to Lovelace's rape is Emma's insult to Miss Bates. In retribution Emma is lectured by Mr. Knightley, and the grounds for his disapproval are quite explicit:

> "Were she a woman of fortune. . . . Were she your equal in situation—but, Emma, consider how far this is from being the case. She is poor; she has sunk from the comforts she was born to; . . . Her situation should secure your compassion. It was badly done, indeed!—You, whom she had known from an infant, whom she had seen grow up from a period when her notice was an honour, to have you now, in thoughtless spirits, and the pride of the moment, laugh at her, humble her—and before her niece, too—and before others, many of whom (certainly *some*), would be entirely guided by *your* treatment of her."

Emma's fault, though never in doubt, is measured in terms of the particular circumstances and people involved. The scale must be smaller in *Emma* because growth is a diminution, a movement from the heroic to the human.

The true perfection of Clarissa has become the self-deception of Emma. Clarissa has no imagination because she is truly a heroine. She is the woman above reproach encountering the man beneath contempt. She doesn't need imagination because her own experience is incredibly exciting and the criteria of judgment have been provided for her. There are stirring adventures and dark, dark deeds. Emma, however, does not live in a landscape of heroism. She is too flawed and too modern to be a true heroine, and so tries to create heroines of her own. In Austen's novel objective conventions are internalized as mental creations and fact is made fiction. The movement from *Clarissa* to *Emma* can be seen as one from presenting heroic qualities as real to acknowledging them as fictions. Emma is deluded in seeing Harriet or Jane as heroines, and must move out from such fancies into the factual world. Emma needs her imagination not to create fantasies, but to take her out of them into a clear perception of objective reality.

The process of moving outside oneself is a familiar theme in early nineteenth-century English poetry. Robert Langbaum discusses it (with Wordsworth as the example) in language strikingly appropriate to *Emma*:

> For subjectivity was not the program but the inescapable condition of romanticism. No sooner had the eighteenth century left the individual isolated within himself—without an objective counterpart for the values he senses in his own will and feelings—than romanticism began as a movement toward objectivity, toward a new principle of connection with society and nature through the imposition of values on the external world. . . . The whole conscious concern with objectivity as a *problem*, as something to be achieved, is in fact specifically romantic.

And the view of this process as a movement from self-love to love of others through imagination is discussed by Walter Jackson Bate:

> Self-love is an effect rather than a cause, and arises when the individual has a clearer and more vivid idea, through direct experience, of his own "identity" than of the identities of others. But if the imagination is sufficiently wide and intense in its working, he may attain an equally clear and vigorous idea of the "identity" of another—an idea which, according as it is supported by intelligent and attentive observation, becomes

> transmuted into a sympathetic feeling of proportionate justness, and results in a consequent moral concern as strong as self-love, if not stronger.

Bate, far from referring to Jane Austen, is describing the theme of Hazlitt's *Principles of Human Action*. Yet he could be describing the theme of *Emma*.

Emma is the great English novel of the early nineteenth century. With it the radical changes from eighteenth-century moral and aesthetic conventions which were appearing in poetry with Wordsworth also appear in fiction. The reader's major responsibility is not that of distinguishing the truth from Emma's version of it (i.e., separating Emma from Austen). That discrimination is essential but secondary. The primary activity is that provided for the reader by the artistic technique—the act of directly seeing into the consciousness of someone else. The process of understanding through the immediacy of experience supersedes judgment as a moral act. Getting to know Emma from the inside doesn't mitigate or transform our judgment. This is not a matter of objective justice qualified by subjective forgiveness. Judgment emerges from the special experience of seeing as Emma sees, because that experience, that being someone else, is the moral of the story. Emma's belated offer of arrowroot to Jane has deep connections with Wordsworth's sense of harmony with men and nature through "the meanest flower that blows."

The Importance of Being Frank

John Peter Rumrich

Frank Churchill charges the staid world of Highbury with social and emotional life, but receives little recognition for his service. One critic even goes so far as to say that he "embodies the depravity of France." Like Emma, critics find Frank lacking when they compare him to George Knightley. Yet, despite his faults, Frank holds a vital structural post in the plot but escapes the fate germane to most structurally indispensable characters, that of being merely a formal necessity, a mechanism. In fact, I maintain that Jane Austen finds in Frank a brilliant solution to the crucial problem of *Emma*—how to bring constructive change and a new order to the novel when she is confronted with Emma and the petrified world of Highbury.

Mr. Elton performs a role similar to Churchill's in that volume 1 rests on Emma's failure to see through him, much as the rest of the story depends on her blindness about Frank. A would-be charm boy who attempts to flatter the rich Miss Woodhouse into loving or marrying him, Elton fails in his labors and subsequently reveals a spiteful nature capable of much petty malice. Smugly satisfied in his own presumptuous cleverness, this sychophant earns our just contempt through most of *Emma*, and even the still-fooled Miss Woodhouse can scarcely contain her inclination to laugh at the "parade in his speeches." It seems to me that volume 1 suffers when compared to the rest of the work as a consequence of Elton's grasping insufficiency. Possibilities appear not to exist in the mechanical world of volume 1. Once the cog opposed to Emma

---

From *Essays in Literature* 8, no. 1 (Spring 1981).

has made his turns—entirely fathomable turns, not funny or charming nor nasty enough to arouse morbid curiosity—he ceases to occupy us at all. Emma, moreover, suffers from her proximity to him because she spends so much of herself merely in complementing his turns. What feeling we do have for her in volume 1 Knightley tags as "an anxiety, a curiosity," but by no means does she command attention and affectionate sympathy as she later does.

Mr. Elton's inadequacy becomes dramatically obvious when the Westons hold their Christmas party. As she enters Randalls, Emma wants only "to enjoy all that was enjoyable to the utmost." As a condition for that happiness, she resolves "to think as little as possible of Mr. Elton's oddities, or of anything else unpleasant." The officious lover nevertheless becomes an obstacle to all her expected enjoyment as he sits "at her elbow," "continually obtruding his happy countenance on her notice, and solicitously addressing her upon every occasion." *Emma* stands still until the vicar leaves center stage. Emma's feelings accurately parallel those of a frustrated reader: "She could not be rude . . . she was even positively civil; but it was an effort; especially as something was going on amongst the others, in the most overpowering period of Mr. Elton's nonsense, which she particularly wished to listen to. She heard enough to know that Mr. Weston was giving some information about his son . . . but before she could quiet Mr. Elton, the subject was . . . past." We care to see no more of Elton, nor of his labored complaisance. Austen carts him off to his appropriate marital fate—a coggified Emma.

Churchill we do want to see. He promises rescue from the stuffy Elton plot. For Emma he promises rescue from a society which saps her vitality. Emma typically allows no situation to bloom into forthright expression as she attempts to make life smooth both for herself and for her father, smooth as the ideal bowl of gruel. Accepting the resultant anxiety as her lot, she spends herself in the manipulation of volatile combinations of people and places away from openness, anger, joy, or any of those unbalanced states through which people grow and learn. And yet, despite her delusions about how things must be and how pleasant such a predetermined condition will be, Emma cannot stifle the tremor of honest excitement triggered by the mere mention of Frank Churchill:

> Now, it so happened that in spite of Emma's resolution of never marrying, there was something in the name, in the idea of Mr. Frank Churchill, which always interested her. She had frequently thought—especially since his father's marriage with

> Miss Taylor—that if she *were* to marry, he was the very person to suit her in age, character and condition. . . . and though not meaning to be induced by him, or by anybody else, to give up a situation which she believed more replete with good than any she could change it for, she had a great curiosity to see him.

Void of Elton's smothering sameness, Churchill acts as a harbinger of change to Highbury. He promotes open-ended situations. His free and charming manner has "no air of study or exaggeration." As paradoxical as it might seem when one considers the mystery he authors, Frank indeed is frank. His actions and attitudes contrast strikingly with the social constraint practiced by most others in Highbury. Exactly opposite to Mr. Woodhouse in lifestyle and in effect on others, Frank is the only person for whom the torpid valetudinarian expresses anything near dislike—Frank, alas, "is not quite the thing." Emma's father cannot abide choices, possibilities, movement or anything at all having to do with imbalance. He lives, or stays alive, "hating change of every kind" and believing "matrimony, as the origin of change," to be "always disagreeable."

Frank, on the other hand, pushes situations to disequilibrium. Highbury has not seen a ball in years, but when Frank visits, a ball takes place. The possibility of dancing never arises without his presence and upon his departure plans for the ball rest literally in a state of suspended animation. After Frank leaves town, Emma concludes that she must love him because of "the sensation of listlessness, weariness, stupidity" which overcomes her, "this feeling of everything's being dull and insipid about the house." Her feelings do not, however, attest to love; rather, they outline Churchill's effect. Emma misses the vitality, the aura of anticipation he brings to her world. Frank conjures what George Santayana calls "the spirit of comedy" and, as Emma's sense of loss indicates, "where the spirit of comedy has departed, company becomes constraint, reserve eats up the spirit, and people fall into a penurious melancholy in their scruple always to be exact, sane, and reasonable, never to mourn, never to glow, never to betray a passion or a weakness, nor venture to utter a thought they might not wish to harbour forever." The scene now belongs to another visitor. Mr. John Knightley, whose "grave looks and reluctant conversations" indeed promise a "penurious melancholy."

As Austen's agent for change, Frank moves on behalf of love and marriage, and, in general, for succession from the dying old to the living new—from the stale rigidity of Mr. Woodhouse and Mrs. Churchill to the fresh flexibility of the newlyweds who emerge at the end. He does not, however, represent "the purposeless desire for change." On the contrary, he reaffirms the social order by introducing a new Mrs. Churchill to Enscombe, one who will better the old in true gentility. Thus Frank upholds the manners due Miss Fairfax's worth and fumes at the overweening Mrs. Elton's use of the familiar "Jane." Comedy, as many have said, likes to conserve the natural order and subverts only the unnatural, the sterile, those who would try to maintain things always the same, and always the way they want them. Frank, therefore, lives disguised to stay near his lady and thwart the powerful dominance which would strike against his love.

Critical outcry against Frank stems from comparing him to Knightley in a moral perspective. Taking their lead from Emma, and from what they suppose Austen valued, many readers fall "naturally into a comparison" and acclaim "Mr. Knightley's high superiority of character." Judgment in favor of Knightley seems proper when it comes from Emma, but the novel itself allows and even insists upon a larger view (thus irony). When we look from one perspective only, we imitate Emma's father who never can understand "that other people could feel differently from himself." Emphasis in *Emma* repeatedly falls on the importance of openness to others' views—"evil to some is always good to others," as Emma herself says. Consequently, as she again tells us, "one half the world cannot understand the pleasures of the other." Mr. Knightley holds, for example, that "surprizes are foolish things; the pleasure is not enhanced, and the inconvenience is often considerable." But any child would disagree, and Austen quickly undercuts our hero as happy dancers move to the music of the new pianoforte: "the rarity and suddeness of it"—the narrator makes sure to describe the situation so—make this particular surprise "very delightful." Who qualifies as judge between the Knightleys and the Churchills? Jane Austen perhaps would have preferred a Knightley, but she certainly valued the Churchills of the world.

Still, Austen appears to encourage the use of moralizing spectacles when we look at Frank. Although we hear about him from the beginning, we do not see him until much later. Like Emma, we reach the point where we will "not be satisfied unless he comes." Emma's own expectations, and indeed, all of Highbury's intensify our desire to meet Frank. The author has Churchill disappoint these expectations, thus adding to our suspense and efficiently characterizing Frank in his absence. Hence, he remains outside of Highbury for well over a third of the novel, and then enters into a pre-existing set of questions which have been posed concerning his behavior. The questions fall into two related groups: does he want to visit Highbury or not; and, if he does, what does his continued absence signify? These questions limit the possible answers as rendered from Knightley's moral position. If he does not care to visit, then he must be "proud, luxurious, and selfish." If he does want to visit, but does not because of family pressures, then he must be too weak a man to follow the commands of "duty." As things turn out, he probably does not care to visit Highbury until after Jane Fairfax arrives. But he does not fit easily into the confines of Knightley's derogatory adjectives.

When Knightley comments on Frank's offenses against the "strict rule of right," he faults him for standing "too much indebted to the event for his acquittal." The magisterial Mr. Knightley, however, never defends himself against the countercharge tacitly levelled by the novel's conclusion. After all, without the intervention of poultry pilferers, Emma and Knightley's marriage might never have come off. No one in Highbury, it seems, except perhaps Frank's father, does justice to the power of events. No one there appreciates an event as Frank does, least of all Mr. Knightley. They fail to understand the comic life, a life whose principal tenet states that "all creatures live by opportunities in a world fraught with disasters." Mr. Weston and son, so often described as sanguine, rely on the belief "that if things are going untowardly one month, they are sure to mend the next." One may easily fear events, as Mr. Woodhouse does, for they do not always occur as one supposes. Easy, too, is the pretense that certain rules always hold, that certain causes always bring on certain effects. Emma painfully learns the contrary in volume 3 when she asks if it is "new for any thing in this world to be unequal, inconsistent, incongruous—or for chance and circumstance (as second causes) to direct the human fate?" Even Knightley sometimes comes to the wrong conclusion. He should not begin so many sentences with the phrase "depend upon it."

Events help to bring Emma and Knightley closer despite themselves, and Frank Churchill occupies an integral position in these events. His return to Highbury opens Emma to thoughts of marriage, of spring: "she wished she might be able to keep him from an absolute declaration . . . and yet she could not help rather anticipating something decisive. She felt as if the spring would not pass without bringing a crisis, an event, a something to alter her present composed and tranquil state." Emma appreciates her destined mate more when Frank visits than she ever does in his absence; she continually compares Knightley with him until she finally realizes that she loves Knightley. Frank's flirtation with Emma also helps Knightley to recognize his feelings for Emma —"he had been in love with Emma, and jealous of Frank Churchill, from about the same period, one sentiment having probably enlightened him as to the other."

Prior to Frank's entrance, Emma aims to spend her days in the twilight of caring for her father in his perpetual round of gruel, backgammon and sleep. Her own "resources" (as Mrs. Elton later echoes) will occupy her, a sort of emotional and social masturbation. Knightley, without the push Frank provides, would remain within the confines of a stodgy bachelorhood highlighted by account taking with Will Larkin. Fortunately, Knightley acts from impulse when he proposes. Attempts to create love—even by Knightley—do not often succeed. Living for once in the moment, Emma and Knightley leave behind worries about old Mr. Woodhouse and scruples about characteristic anti-marriage stances. Their garden meeting and betrothal partakes of timeless love comedy, with value recognized on each side, hearts appropriately humbled and open, and nature sympathetically surrounding them with warmth and beauty. Interwoven with the time and situation, the event, is Frank Churchill. References to him punctuate their conversation and the narrative frame; Austen summarizes Knightley's shift in attitude by registering his changing feelings toward Frank. Perhaps they would have fallen in love without Frank's influence, but Jane Austen, at least, needed him to accomplish the feat.

What, then, are we to do with Frank Churchill? He does not fit into any pre-arranged categories; and characters' opinions of him often change —and change according to their own fluctuations, not Frank's. Knightley's final moral judgment of him—"Faults of inconsideration and thoughtlessness"—cannot, from his strict moral viewpoint, be argued. Nor can it help us to understand Frank's impact on the novel. If his moral flaws lightened our understanding of his actions, we could solve the problem of his character and understand him much as we do Elton. If we could do so, however, a close reading of the novel would not entertain or intrigue so powerfully. The novel would once again become a moral machine, an ironic caricature. Because of Churchill's authenticity and consequent indeterminacy, we cannot help but wonder what he is about. The most accurate descriptions of him all express this incomprehensibility:

> Emma perceived that the nature of his gallantry was a little self-willed, and that he would rather oppose than lose the

> pleasure of dancing with her. . . . Had she intended ever to *marry* him it might have been worth while to pause and consider, and try to understand the value of his preference, and the character of his temper.
>
> This gallant young man . . . seemed to love without feeling, and to recommend himself without complaisance.
>
> Jane was forced to smile completely, for a moment; and the smile partly remained as she turned towards him, and said in a conscious, low, yet steady voice,
>
> "How you can bear such recollections, is astonishing to me! They *will* sometimes obtrude—but how you can *court* them!"

We hear in these lines a hint of the outrage elicited by some of Frank's more embarrassing and morally inexcusable traits. But, aside from this note of justifiable indignation, we also recognize the admission of a paradox—as if the characters concerned were throwing up their hands and stepping back to consider one of life's mysteries.

Questions and paradoxes collect around Frank in a book filled with puzzles, conundrums and mysteries because he reflects, I believe, the author's own sense of wonder at the way things happen. Frank stands before us palpable, waiting to be understood or accepted. Despite his open character, many readers suspect him of hidden motives—perhaps evil ones. But the man himself, regardless of his plot-producing secret, exists without concealed luggage waiting to spill open and reveal his true motivation. Frank simply is the way he acts. Jane Austen presents us with Elton and Churchill: one cleverly designed and motivated for his spot in an exact machine; and the other born alive in the author's imagination, a comic interloper whose character reflects Austen's living solution to the story of *Emma*, a comedy.

As the author's comic inspiration, Frank neither fears the future nor regrets the past. Never could he bear the married life Emma anticipates: "such a companion," she muses about Knightley, "in the periods of anxiety and cheerlessness before her!—Such a partner in all those duties and cares to which time must be giving increase of melancholy!" Frank sees nothing in the conflicting paths the future might hold except "every possibility of good." His explanatory letter, often thought an oily dodge, really does provide a key to his behavior: "you will be ready to say, what was your hope in doing this?—What did you look forward to?—To any thing, every thing—to time, chance, circumstances, slow effects, sudden bursts, perseverance, and weariness, health and sickness." Keeping dread a stranger, Frank pushes situations to their limits, and hopes that events will unite him with Jane. Thus he creates and exploits social moments; because he does, his own romance flourishes and the novel ends happily. Although Frank's treatment of Jane Fairfax may be justly condemned, we must recognize that his apparent cruelty to his fiancée is consistent with—even a consequence of—his special role in the novel. Jane herself ultimately refuses to blame Frank because, as she says, "I did not make all the allowances . . . which I ought to have done, for his temper and spirits—his delightful spirits, and that gaity, that playfulness of disposition, which, under any other circumstances, would, I am sure, have been constantly bewitching . . . as they were at first." Despite the real discomfort he causes her, Frank loves Jane and frees her from a bleak economic prison. One might even suggest that his unabashed enjoyment of life seems precisely the sort of influence Jane needs to overcome what Knightley calls, with characteristic understatement, a lack of the "open temper which a man would wish for in a wife." Knightley's understatement finds balance, appropriately in Emma's characteristic overstatement—she finds Jane "disgustingly . . . suspiciously reserved." With any luck, and what could be more customary than luck for "the child of good fortune," Frank and Jane will complement each other as Knightley and Emma do.

George Santayana's "The Comic Mask" proposes a creative attitude toward living which Frank Churchill in many ways exemplifies. The Frank I have attempted to identify appears in the following lines from that essay:

> Moralists have habitually aimed at suppression, wisely perhaps at first . . . but why continue to harp on propriety and unselfishness . . . when we . . . have hardly any self or any passions left to indulge? Perhaps the time has come to suspend those exhortations. . . . We should then be living in the spirit of comedy, and the world would grow young. Every occasion would don its comic mask, and make its bold grimace at the world for a moment. We should be constantly original without effort and without shame, somewhat as we are in dreams, and consistent only in sincerity; and we should gloriously emphasize all the poses we fell into, without seeking to prolong them!

Whether Jane Austen would agree with my estimation of Frank's character can never be known, but she certainly would allow that the last two-thirds of *Emma* takes a good part of its life from him. Miss Woodhouse and Mr. Knightley find each other in the presence of this comic catalyst. And their union, after all, is the happy ending's essence.

Even during a second reading, when we know what Frank will do next, we do not lose interest. In the human context of social behavior he feels life and calls it forth—even plays with it. Unlike most of the characters in *Emma*, he does not often laugh at someone or something; he does not laugh with derision but with pleasure. The apparent paradox which the narrator cites—a man who loves "without feeling" and recommends "himself without complaisance"—does not condemn Frank, nor does it approve of him. It simply is a mark of wonder. Somewhere within the character of "that perfect novelty," Mr. Frank Churchill, underneath the eighteenth-century gentleman, a tinge of Dionysian revelry pertains; an intimation of the comic spirit whispers to us—a spirit which can visit the static mechanism of Highbury life and transform it into a dance. And although "it may be possible to do without dancing entirely . . . when the felicities of rapid motion have once been, though slightly, felt—it must be a very heavy set that does not ask for more."

A Comedy of Intimacy

Jan Fergus

Emma is a comedy more of intimacy than of judgment, though judgment of character is so frequently at issue in the novel and though the plot is brilliantly constructed to challenge and exercise the reader's judgment. Because intimacy is the special intention of *Emma*, it dictates many details of composition, including the need to portray a close, small world like Highbury faithfully and exhaustively. The society of Highbury, its amusements, its interests, its daily routines, must all be made familiar to the reader. Most important is the need to make characters known, and Austen fulfils this need through conversations in which the characters make themselves known as they discuss themselves or others. These conversations are enormously complex as a result. No analysis can exhaust the implications or connections of even the briefest of them, for everything in *Emma* reflects on everything else. The novel presents readers with a perfectly smooth, taut, rounded surface; its integrity is like that of a sphere, offering criticism no handles. Nevertheless, some of the techniques which allow Austen to create a world of such fullness and intricacy are visible in the conversation from the early chapter in which Mr Knightley and Mrs Weston discuss Emma.

The most important of these techniques is simple and direct: Austen promotes intimacy between her readers and her characters by creating characters who are intimate with each other and whose speech reflects their intimacy. Mr Knightley and Mrs Weston know Emma well, and

From *Jane Austen and the Didactic Novel*: Northanger Abbey, Sense and Sensibility, *and* Pride and Prejudice. Barnes & Noble Books, 1983.

what they say of her reflects both their affection and their knowledge of her, faults and all. They also know each other so well that earlier in the scene they can openly discuss what might seem an impossibly rude, threatening or painful subject: Mr Knightley's disapproval of Mrs Weston as a governess for Emma. Mrs Weston says, most directly, "I am sure you always thought me unfit for the office I held," and Mr Knightley's reply is even more direct. "Yes," said he, smiling. "You are better placed *here*; very fit for a wife, but not at all for a governess." Mr Knightley's smile indicates the affectionate intimacy that saves his remark from harshness, and Mrs Weston is not at all offended. That their intimacy is perfectly reciprocal is clear when Mrs Weston corrects him later in the scene and he accepts her correction with good grace. She advises him not to discuss with Mr John Knightley or Isabella his disapproval of Emma's "intimacy" with Harriet Smith, as she does not "think any possible good" will be achieved. She continues,

> "It has been so many years my province to give advice, that you cannot be surprized, Mr Knightley, at this little remains of office."
>
> "Not at all," cried he; "I am much obliged to you for it. It is very good advice, and it shall have a better fate than your advice has often found; for it shall be attended to."
>
> "Mrs John Knightley is easily alarmed, and might be made unhappy about her sister."
>
> "Be satisfied," said he, "I will not raise any outcry. I will keep my ill-humour to myself. I have a very sincere interest in Emma. Isabella does not seem more my sister; has never excited a greater interest; perhaps hardly so great. There is an anxiety, a curiosity in what one feels for Emma I wonder what will become of her!"
>
> "So do I," said Mrs Weston gently; "very much."
>
> "She always declares she will never marry, which, of course, means just nothing at all. But I have no idea that she has yet ever seen a man she cared for. It would not be a bad thing for her to be very much in love with a proper object. I should like to see Emma in love, and in some doubt of a return; it would do her good. But there is nobody hereabouts to attach her; and she goes so seldom from home."

This passage, brief as it is and simple by comparison to any exchange in which Emma herself participates, bears an ironic relation to almost all of the plot. Mr Knightley is not yet aware of his own love for Emma, and when she later shows an interest in Frank Churchill even before meeting him, Mr Knightley's hostility and jealousy reveal to himself his love for her. "He had been in love with Emma, and jealous of Frank Churchill, from about the same period, one sentiment having probably enlightened him as to the other." So far from liking "to see Emma in love, and in some doubt of a return," when he suspects "a something of private liking, of private understanding even, between Frank Churchill and Jane," a liking that would threaten Emma if she loves Frank, he attempts to warn her, for "He could not see her in a situation of such danger, without trying to preserve her." More ironic still, when Emma actually is in love with a proper object (Mr Knightley himself), and in some doubt of a return, it *does* do her good, for it makes her "understand the deceptions she had been thus practising on herself, and living under! – The blunders, the blindness of her own head and heart!"

A kind of linear irony is at work here, although the term seems increasingly inadequate for the connections between this passage and others in the novel. Linear irony implies reversal, which does not really describe what happens between Mr Knightley's ambiguously phrased declaration that "Isabella does not seem more my sister" and his later very moving response when Emma invites him to dance, saying, "You have shown that you can dance, and you know we are not really so much brother and sister as to make it at all improper." "Brother and sister! no, indeed." This exchange is highly charged with feeling because of the incongruity between Mr Knightley's now conscious love for Emma and her still unconscious love for him. His denial of a fraternal relation to her reflects back on his earlier remark poignantly rather than ironically or comically. The reader should note too that Emma's words here are phrased ambiguously, quite like his earlier ones. Even when both are unaware of their love, they are far from ready to see themselves as brother and sister.

A less powerful connection but an important one exists also between Mr Knightley's willingness to keep his ill-humour to himself and such incidents as Emma's readiness to repress her discontent when Mr Weston injudiciously invites Mrs Elton to join their expedition to Box Hill:

> so it was to be, if she had no objection. Now, as her objection was nothing but her very great dislike of Mrs Elton, of which Mr Weston must already be perfectly aware, it was not worth

> bringing forward again:—it could not be done without a reproof to him, which would be giving pain to his wife; and she found herself therefore obliged to consent to an arangement which she would have done a great deal to avoid; an arrangement which would probably expose her even to the degradation of being said to be of Mrs Elton's party! Every feeling was offended; and the forbearance of her outward submission left a heavy arrear due of secret severity in her reflections on the unmanageable good-will of Mr Weston's temper.

Touches like these make *Emma* the miracle it is. The complexity of response required of a reader is immense. He must register Emma's faults and virtues at every line, for her snobbery and her consideration are perfectly intermixed. The reader also, sharing Emma's hearty dislike of Mrs Elton, will be equally indignant at Mr Weston's "unmanageable good-will," and is as likely as Emma to wish some outlet for this indignation. But annoyance, irritation, ill-humour and indignation are not allowed free expression: they must not be permitted to hurt others. Forbearance is, therefore, of great value in this novel, although not the greatest. Emma's forbearance here is admirable, and does make one love her. In this scene, however, she is forbearing, not loving or good-natured, and forbearance can give way under stress, as Emma's does at Box Hill, allowing her to insult Miss Bates. Love, a higher and more generous sentiment, is required. Emma's love for her father, who is a clear foil to Miss Bates, makes forbearance unnecessary or irrelevant in her relations with him, although his demands on her are ceaseless and his selfish fretfulness far more irritating than Miss Bates's verbosity. Mr Knightley's readiness to suppress his ill-humour in the early scene thus announces a theme which will be sounded and varied again and again in *Emma*, reaching a climax at Box Hill. Similarly, his ready acceptance of advice echoes another important motif, for giving and taking advice are frequently at issue, whether Emma is advising Harriet or being advised by Mr Knightley.

Austen uses the dialogue between Mr Knightley and Mrs Weston to create other, more immediate effects on the reader than linear irony allows. One such effect is produced when Mr Knightley declares that "there is nobody hereabouts to attach" Emma. His comments on her in all of chapter 5 ostensibly declare him an affectionate friend with no other idea in mind. He considers that she has never yet seen anyone she could care for. Austen guards against the reader's anticipating the conclusion too soon by allowing Mr Knightley thus to ignore the possibility that he could be Emma's suitor; the reader is made more likely to ignore it also. Yet Mr Knightley's ignorance is no unfair trick to mislead the reader. His unconscious love for Emma is not merely necessary to the plot but perfectly consistent with the history of his relation to her. When Mr Knightley claims, on the other hand, that "There is an anxiety, a curiosity in what one feels for Emma. I wonder what will become of her," Austen's intentions are different. She is allowing him to articulate the central issue of the novel. What one feels for Emma is as important, page by page, as the unfolding of her character and destiny, and Austen is using Mr Knightley's speech in the simplest, most direct way to guide the reader's attention to the question of his own response to Emma. The speeches of Mr Knightley and Mrs Weston also, in an unobtrusive way, give some information about Emma's early history, which helps the reader to understand, allow for and feel for her character, particularly the information that "ever since she was twelve, Emma has been mistress of the house and of you all." What Mr Knightley and Mrs Weston say also has other effects on the reader's response to Emma. Their speeches voice their different estimations of her character and conduct (especially of her intimacy with Harriet Smith) and require the reader to judge between them. This use of conversation is, however, more conventional and less daring than its use as a kind of aside to the reader, reminding him of his task. Mr Knightley's mentioning "an anxiety, a curiosity" in one's feelings for Emma is rather like Edmund Bertram's declaring to Fanny that "There is no reason in the world why you should not be important where you are known." Both statements are addressed to the reader as much as to Mrs Weston or Fanny.

The effects any passage in *Emma* has upon a reader's perceptions and judgments are difficult to separate from both emotional and comic effects. Techniques and their effects are much less obvious than in *Pride and Prejudice*: what is the effect, for instance, on a second reading, of Mr Knightley's ignorance of his own heart in chapter 5? Some amusement is certainly felt at the discrepancy between this ignorance and his decided, definite pronouncements about his feelings for Emma and indeed about everything else. Yet this amusement is qualified; his ignorance comes to seem painful, as it leads to his difficult position as observer of Emma's flirtation with Frank Churchill. Thus, his response to Mrs Weston's praise of Emma's beauty creates an almost indefinable effect. He says first, "I confess that I have seldom seen a face or figure more pleasing to me than her's. But I am a partial old friend," and then more powerfully,

"I love to look at her." The incongruity between what he acknowledges to himself and what he really feels, between so much open and so much concealed affection, is intensely moving. Certainly the effect is not like that produced when Elizabeth Bennet tells Darcy, "It is particularly incumbent on those who never change their opinion, to be secure of judging properly at first," even though Elizabeth's remark is not purely comic either. The different effects seem attributable to the higher emotional content which informs and underlies dialogue in the later novels. Unacknowledged or suppressed love is a major theme in them all, along with an investigation of its consequences.

Concealment in general is also prominent in *Emma*. Mrs Weston's reply to Mr Knightley's comments about wishing to see Emma in love is oblique, for "Part of her meaning was to conceal some favourite thoughts of her own and Mr Weston's on the subject, as much as possible. There were wishes at Randalls respecting Emma's destiny, but it was not desirable to have them suspected." These thoughts are of a marriage between Frank Churchill and Emma, thoughts Emma herself entertains. It is typical of Austen's practice in *Emma* that she should end this scene, which has expressed so much openness, goodwill and intimacy, with some slight obliquity and reserve. As Austen comments later, when Emma has received Mr Knightley's declaration of love, and is obliged to conceal both her former fear that he loved Harriet, and Harriet's existing attachment, "Seldom, very seldom, does complete truth belong to any human disclosure; seldom can it happen that something is not a little disguised, or a little mistaken; but where, as in this case, though the conduct is mistaken, the feelings are not, it may not be very material."

This passage has been sometimes taken as evidence that Austen acknowledges an almost modern consciousness of human isolation and of the impossibility of knowing or being known. On the contrary: the whole thrust of *Emma* is toward openness, knowledge and intimacy. The limits or restrictions which human nature dictates for these qualities (limits the novels fully concede) are less interesting to Austen than are their possibilities in human relations. Once Emma hears that Harriet is engaged to Robert Martin,

> High in the rank of her most serious and heartfelt felicities, was the reflection that all necessity of concealment from Mr Knightley would soon be over. The disguise, equivocation, mystery, so hateful to her to practise, might soon be over. She

> could now look forward to giving him that full and perfect confidence which her disposition was most ready to welcome as a duty.

This passage carries more weight within *Emma* than its counterpart, reinforced as it is by the very moving, open, intimate conversations between Mr Knightley and Emma after their engagement.

The plot of *Emma* moves toward the release and acknowledgement of concealed love, and the result is intimacy. The secret engagement of Jane Fairfax and Frank Churchill is revealed and all the mystification associated with it dispelled, just as the unconscious love of Emma and Mr Knightley is made conscious. In the process the plot takes in a great deal more, including Emma's misconduct, her various stages of repentance, and her relapses, all of which have complicated effects in controlling the reader's judgment of her and sympathy for her. Yet the emphasis on judgment, enhanced as it is by the central mystery tantalizingly presented for the reader to make out, is oddly undercut at the end, making *Emma* the comedy of intimacy that it is, not a comedy of judgment.

Frank Churchill, for example, has conducted himself in the novel so as to invite and deserve the reader's harshest criticism. He too parodies Emma's worst qualities, for he fools and manipulates everyone. Emma says to him at last, "I think there is a little likeness between us," but in fact Frank is much worse than Emma. He is irresponsible and thoughtless. He torments Jane, whom he loves. When his duplicity and cruelty are first revealed, Emma's righteous indignation is most welcome to the reader and voices his own judgment of Frank's conduct: "Impropriety! Oh! Mrs Weston—it is too calm a censure. Much, much beyond impropriety!—It has sunk him, I cannot say how it has sunk him in my opinion. So unlike what a man should be!—None of that upright integrity, that strict adherence to truth and principle, that disdain of trick and littleness, which a man should display in every transaction of his life." Emma is, of course, thinking unconsciously of Mr Knightley as she speaks, and a little of her own impropriety in suspecting an attachment between Jane and Mr Dixon and then in imparting that suspicion to Frank. Every judgment in *Emma* is qualified by self-regarding consideration like these. Nevertheless, Emma's indignation is meant to be felt as the first in a series of judgments of Frank Churchill's character, judgments whose reversals undercut moral judgment in general and Emma's, Mr Knightley's and the reader's in particular.

Emma herself is soon forced by Mrs Weston to "listen better" to excuses for Frank, and is in any case quickly taken up with her own concerns (thinking Frank's uncle would have consented as readily to a marriage with Harriet as with Jane). The summary of Mr Knightley's response to Frank's engagement offers an even finer and more sustained joke on moral judgment than does the course of Emma's first response: "He had found [Emma] agitated and low. – Frank Churchill was a villain. – He heard her declare that she had never loved him. Frank Churchill's character was not desperate. – She was his own Emma, by hand and word, when they returned into the house; and if he could have thought of Frank Churchill then, he might have deemed him a very good sort of fellow." This response finds an echo in Emma's later reaction to Frank Churchill's letter of explanation: "though it was impossible not to feel that he had been wrong, yet he had been less wrong than she had supposed – and he had suffered, and was very sorry – and he was so grateful to Mrs Weston, and so much in love with Miss Fairfax, and she was so happy herself, that there was no being severe; and could he have entered the room, she must have shaken hands with him as heartily as ever." This letter has much the same softening effect on the reader as on Emma, and so Mr Knightley is brought back again to provide one more reversal as he goes over it, revealing in his stringent comments what the reader and Emma should have thought. And yet Mr Knightley's heart is hardly in the subject. He doesn't want to read the letter in the first place, cuts short his judgment, and proceeds to talk with Emma of their marriage: "I have another person's interest at present so much at heart, that I cannot think any longer about Frank Churchill."

The didactic effect of *Emma* is a complicated one. The reader's judgment is evoked, beguiled, confounded, refined and then dissolved or transcended by love. Even more is required of his sympathies. Miss Bates, for example, is so perfectly rendered in her tiresome verbosity that Walter Scott's review cites Austen's treatment as a fault: "Characters of folly or simplicity, such as those of old Woodhouse and Miss Bates, are ridiculous when first presented, but if too often brought forward or too long dwelt upon, their prosing is apt to become as tiresome in fiction as in real society." Yet Scott's reaction half fulfills Austen's intention. Unless Miss Bates iyfelt as boring, even irritating, and unless the reader is to that extent implicated in Emma's insult at Box Hill, one part of the effect of that splendid scene is lost.

At Box Hill, all the sexual and social tension, irritation and frustration that the action has generated explodes. The reader is made to know what every character is feeling during the scene partly through dialogue and narrative, and partly through the knowledge of each that the novel has so carefully imparted. The amount and kind of bad feeling expressed, the incongruity between every character's feelings and motives, the various ways in which each partly understands and partly mistakes the others, are all astonishing. Emma's much-cited insult to Miss Bates is not surprising in the context of so much bad feeling, and yet it is shocking. Almost as shocking is Mr Weston's conundrum, which immediately follows: "What two letters of the alphabet are there, that express perfection? . . . M. and A.—Em—ma.—Do you understand?" The juxtaposition of Emma's most unkind act and Mr Weston's tribute is a touch typical of *Emma*. Yet the scene does not stop here, as in a sense it should; it keeps going, and the reader's attention is absorbed by the ugliness which follows, most notably Frank Churchill's declaration to Emma that when he returns from abroad, "I shall come to you for my wife," a flirtatious remark aimed at Jane Fairfax that seems to her to be serious courtship of Emma, and to Emma a "commission" to groom Harriet for the post, for deluded as she is otherwise, Emma does know that Frank Churchill's gallantry to her "now, in her own estimation, meant nothing." Indeed, the reader would be in as much danger as Emma of overlooking her rudeness without Mr Knightley's rebuke. His words to Emma, "How could you be so unfeeling," are addressed in part to the reader, and indeed his words so firmly fix the incident as the central one of the scene, both in Emma's mind and in the reader's, that to reread the chapter and to find Emma's insult buried in so much more obviously ugly interaction is a shock. That Emma is struck and chastened by Mr Knightley's rebuke is clear, not only in the tears she sheds going home, but in her reflections in the evening. "As a daughter, she hoped she was not without a heart. She hoped no one could have said to her, 'How could you be so unfeeling to your father?'" To be "feeling" in the best sense is what *Emma* teaches, and complicated sequences like these account for its extraordinary power to evoke, exasperate, perplex, extend and enlarge the reader's capacity to feel. Austen's attempts to educate the reader's sympathies as well as his judgments have never been so ambitious or so successful.

Gossip

Patricia Meyer Spacks

Jane Austen's *Emma*, dealing with village existence, evokes a society without a "world." The people who talk about one another in Highbury all have faces; reactions from neighbors and friends respond promptly to social deviation. The knowing narrator of the novel, who understands the kinds of restriction implicit in a tiny, intimate society, helps to locate the missing term in her heroine's experience, calling attention to the limitations of Emma's consciousness as well as of her society.

The relation between gossip as social prohibition and as narrative resource becomes explicit here: *Emma* articulates a grammar of gossip. Slightly past the mid-point of the novel, Mr. Knightley explains an important truth to Emma and Mrs. Weston. "Another thing must be taken into consideration too," he observes—"Mrs. Elton does not talk *to* Miss Fairfax as she speaks *of* her. We all know the difference between the pronouns he or she and thou, the plainest-spoken amongst us." The entire novel glosses that difference, and elucidates the further distinction of the first-person pronoun from the others. When Emma violates decorum by talking *to* Miss Bates as she might have spoken *of* her—as a dullard—she prepares the way for a sequence of insights which ends by establishing her in a new relation to the first-person pronoun.

People talk a great deal about other people during *Emma*, for one main reason: to alleviate or forestall boredom. The lack of occupation to which some moralists had attributed the female propensity to gossip afflicts male and female characters alike. Only the male Knightleys

---

From *Gossip*. ©1985 by Patricia Meyer Spacks. Knopf, 1985.

partially escape, John working as a lawyer in London and unable to comprehend the Highbury delight in trivial conversation, and George busy about his estate, willing to gossip with the others but less dependent on gossip as a resource. Unlike Austen's other novels, this one dwells on its own sense of confinement. "Imaginist" though she is, Emma faces a real, not an imaginary, problem in the lack of possibility her community affords. No new people: hence the sensational impact of Frank Churchill. No new things to do or see: hence the momentousness of an expedition to Box Hill or even to Donwell. Emma can play backgammon with her father, she can visit the few familiar people who surround her, she can shop for gloves or ribbons, do needlework or read or practice her music. Repeatedly the text emphasizes Highbury's limitations. At the very beginning, we learn that Emma, "with all her advantages, natural and domestic, . . . was now in great danger of suffering from intellectual solitude." Like everyone around her, she yearns for "news." "Oh! yes, I always like news." The only news available, the only kind relevant to her concerns, involves people she knows or those associated with them. Her impoverished world supplies little else in the way of delight. Walking to the door of a shop while Harriet vacillates over muslins, she seeks

> amusement.—Much could not be hoped from the traffic of even the busiest part of Highbury;—Mr Perry walking hastily by, Mr William Cox letting himself in at the office door, Mr Cole's carriage horses returning from exercise, or a stray letterboy on an obstinate mule, were the liveliest objects she could presume to expect; and when her eyes fell only on the butcher with his tray, a tidy old woman travelling homewards from shop with her full basket, two curs quarrelling over a dirty bone, and a string of dawdling children round the baker's little bow-window eyeing the gingerbread, she knew she had no reason to complain, and was amused enough; quite enough still to stand at the door. A mind lively and at ease can do with seeing nothing, and can see nothing that does not answer.

"A mind lively and at ease." The phrase appears to come from Emma's consciousness; her self-congratulation may recall dreadful Mrs. Elton's talk of her "resources." The liveliness and ease of Emma's mind get her into trouble, as her imagination goes to work on limited raw materials to create gossip which produces false expectations and pain for others. The "he" and "she" who inhabit Emma's imagination belong to the realm of fiction. She constructs shapely plots, domestic romances, about the unmarried; and when she figures as an actress in her own fictions, one begins to understand her difficulty with the first-person pronoun.

From some points of view, Emma seems all too completely at ease with what Virginia Woolf calls the vertical pronoun. Accustomed to rule in her small domain, suffering only the "real evils" of possessing "the power of having rather too much her own way, and a disposition to think a little too well of herself," unchastened by fears of the world, Emma functions insistently as an "I." Yet her version of "I" bears a troubling similarity to her notion of "he" and "she." She sees herself too, repeatedly, as a fictional character, imagining the audience that the village cannot adequately supply. Her entire relationship with Frank Churchill derives from and depends on her capacity to perceive herself from the point of view of admiring spectator. When she and Frank first dance together, "she found herself well-matched in a partner. They were a couple worth looking at." Dwelling as she does on the idea of being looked at, she neglects to recognize what she feels, thinking, rather, of what she might, or should, feel. When Frank reappears, after an absence from Highbury, she concludes that she has not, after all, really fallen in love with him. She gives him, however, "friendly encouragement, . . . which now, in her own estimation, meant nothing, though in the judgment of most people looking on it must have had such an appearance as no English word but flirtation could very well describe. 'Mr Frank Churchill and Miss Woodhouse flirted together excessively.' They were laying themselves open to that very phrase—and to having it sent off in a letter to Maple Grove by one lady, to Ireland by another." This preoccupation with what might be said about her, with, in fact, the gossip she may generate by her self-presentation as well as by her imagination—this preoccupation helps to make possible her thoughtless insult of Miss Bates. She has become so involved in her immediate social role, in her fantasy of being perceived as powerful, witty, and attractive, that she has lost awareness of others' feelings.

Harriet Smith, for all her stupidity and indecisiveness, parodies Emma. She too keeps constructing fictions round herself, less imaginative fictions than Emma specializes in, but constructions in the same genre. She too has trouble knowing her own emotions and accurately assessing other people's. Her failure to function as a full center of consciousness stems from intellectual inadequacy, Emma's, from more complicated sources; but both alike fall into gossip's trap of objectification. Gossip deprives other people of reality; it ends, the novel implies, by doing the same to the self.

Harriet's fictions, of course, in the neat structure of *Austen's* fiction, bring an end to Emma's. When it darts through Emma with the speed of an arrow that Mr. Knightley must marry no one but herself, she moves rapidly from self-dramatization to self-knowledge, toward the marriage that will chasten the excesses of her imagination. She starts now to concentrate on her feelings rather than her performance: to know herself as "I" rather than "she."

Gossip has provided not only an obstacle to the happy ending but a means toward fruition. In the penultimate chapter, Knightley offers Emma a brief account of how the engagement between Harriet Smith and Robert Martin finally came to pass. "This is all that I can relate," he concludes, "of the how, where, and when. Your friend Harriet will make a much longer history when you see her.—She will give you all the minute particulars, which only woman's language can make interesting. —In our communications we deal only in the great." Despite the ironic overtones of Knightley's commentary, he speaks literal truth: woman's language *can* make the trivial and mundane interesting, it can create histories of its own, and it differs from man's language, although men may also employ it. The history Austen has spun out of the daily experience of Highbury precisely demonstrates the point.

Homer Brown has observed, "Traditionally, two of the ways the novel has had of at once disguising and validating itself have been as letters and as gossip. . . . It is probable that part of the pleasure we derive from the classic novel is a pleasure similar to that derived from gossip." Gossip's hermeneutic power generates the internal dynamic of *Emma*: we see its heroine interpreting minute particulars of her own and other people's experience; her acts of interpretation create the plot. Emma exists so completely as an "insider" that "outside" has virtually no existence for her. Her tiny society enables her to function with utter authority; no amount of experience convinces her of her final incapacity to know the meanings of other people's actions within that confined setting. Knightley's condemnation of her rudeness to Miss Bates also derives from the insider's position. In Highbury, one cannot judge people—as, elsewhere, the world does—on the basis of their social performances: one knows too much. Emma should have remembered Miss Bates's history, her personality, her emotional and economic situation. To operate always from inside carries its own penalties—not least of them Emma's inability to distinguish among the pronouns. Her self-objectification declares her yearning for an audience that *will* assess her performance, instead of one for which her performance merges with her history. She yearns, in other words, for a version of that world so threatening to Evelina and other novelistic heroines: the world that would, paradoxically, make her feel more real by fictionizing her.

Gossip carries particularly complex meanings in *Emma* because of the reader's implication in its patterns. The novel consistently invites us too to participate in acts of interpretation. Revealing again and again Emma's interpretive mistakes, giving us the grounds to judge them and her, it may lure us into believing ourselves more competent than she to understand particularities. Guided by the knowing narrator, we can feel ourselves *super*-insiders. The text offers many particularities to understand. When Emma calls on Jane Fairfax shortly after the delivery of her new pianoforte, a gift which, Emma has decided, must come from Mr. Dixon, Jane does not at once sit down at the instrument. "That she was not immediately ready, Emma did suspect to arise from the state of her nerves"; and Emma of course believes herself to understand the proximate cause of nervous tension. The reader possesses the same data as Emma. If we have become, by this point in the novel, wary of Emma's hasty explanations, we face the problem of providing our own. Like a detective novel, the book keeps offering raw material for interpretation, the raw material of gossip, and requiring us to do something with it. The "correct" interpretation for many previous events emerges finally, in the revelation of the secret engagement between Frank and Jane. At this point, we must assess the quality of our own interpretations, realize the degree to which we, as readers, have participated in the making of the fiction—and realize, perhaps, that such participation belongs to a continuum with Highbury's endless speculation. Instead of the pleasure of reading other people's letters, we have been offered the gratifications of complicity—only to have our satisfaction in it repeatedly undermined. Women or not, we have been lured into acting like the women of moralistic stereotypes: lured into rewards and betrayals of speculative gossip. We do not talk out loud, of course; but our inner voices ask gossip's questions, make its judgments.

As usual, Austen provides a conservative text and a challenging subtext. Emma will presumably settle down and behave herself and stop interpreting so wildly; Harriet will stop interpreting at all. The "longer history" of her engagement that Harriet might provide would surely prove tedious in the extreme. Highbury's gossip substitutes for meaningful life; the village's confinement limits growth and pleasure. Although Knightley jokes when he asserts that men "deal only in the great," his superiority to those around him indeed derives partly from his consistent stress on moral rather than merely social judgment. All these facts argue for a view of the novel as supporting values embodied in the moral commentary cited earlier: trivial and malicious talk reflects impoverished minds as well as experience, male talk about ideas communicates more meaning and value than female talk about people; by extension, the male realm provides the standard by which females can judge themselves and know themselves wanting. On the other hand, the vitality of *Emma* as a fiction, like that of Emma as a character, depends on insatiable interest in personality and its individual manifestations. The reader who has found herself or himself amused, entertained, and impressed by the vagaries of Emma's imagination, by her will to make interest where little obvious stuff of interest exists—such a reader must feel the loss involved in Emma's settling down under Mr. Knightley's exemplary tutelage. Emma has kept herself alive while all around decayed, kept herself alive with the energies of gossip. The novel has lured the reader into direct knowledge of the same energies. Talking of "he" and "she" must not substitute for knowing the self as "I" or for valuing the sensibilities of others as "you." On the other hand, the exercise of imagining "he" and "she" and dwelling on the possibilities of their experience enlivens the mind. And recognition of that fact implies at least temporary acceptance of a set of values and assumptions associated with the female and opposed to the usefulness of dealing only in the great. Fully accepting the standards of "society," *Emma* yet declares the need to evade them.

In both *Evelina* and *Emma*, female gossip—literal gossip in the later novel, its written counterpart in the earlier one—functions as a language of feeling, as a mode of personal development, as an evasion of external restriction. Indeed, it becomes a means of discovering selfhood, of declaring the self an expressive, judging consciousness. As a subtext for the major line of narrative, it supports the imaginative and improvisational, valuing the private, implying the saving energies of female curiosity and female volubility, celebrating the possibility and the importance of a narrative of trivia. It exemplifies the subversive resources of the novel as genre. The official criticism of gossip derives from and depends on a realm of public value; it assumes the dominance of "society" as standard and sanction. Novels too declare the importance of society, but they value the individual. Inasmuch as eighteenth-century fiction delineated and defended the private, it often implicitly defended also what public moralists attacked. In fiction if not in didactic texts, the "talent of ready utterance" found its supporters: supporters who managed successfully to uphold the values of a women's sub-society even while articulating those of traditional social conformity. Fiction reveals more clearly what didactic texts only hint: that gossip, "female talk," provides a mode of power, of undermining public rigidities and asserting private integrity, of discovering means of agency for women, those private citizens deprived of public function. It provides also often the substance and the means of narrative.

what public moralists attacked. In fiction if not in didactic texts, the "talent of ready utterance" found its supporters: supporters who managed successfully to uphold the values of a women's subsociety even while articulating those of traditional social conformity. Fiction reveals more clearly what didactic texts only hint: that gossip, "female talk," provides a mode of power, of undermining public rigidities and asserting private integrity, of discovering means of agency for women, those private citizens deprived of public function. It provides also often the substance and the means of narrative.

Reading Characters: Self, Society, and Text in *Emma*

Joseph Litvak

In *The Madwoman in the Attic*, Sandra M. Gilbert and Susan Gubar describe the fate of the Austenian heroine as a "fall into literacy." To fall into literacy is to "fall from authority into the acceptance of one's status as a mere character," to be at once silenced and confined—in the words of one chapter title, to be "Shut Up in Prose." Yet Gilbert and Gubar show how heroines like Elizabeth Bennet, Emma Woodhouse, and Anne Elliot subvert the patriarchal structures in which they are inscribed, imaging Austen's own quiet subversion of the repressive ideology her novels seem to endorse. In reclaiming authority, both Austen and these characters assert their "irrepressible interiority" and their "belief in female subjectivity."

Austen's novels are indeed subtly subversive, but this subversion does not take place in the name of interiority, subjectivity, or even authority, if authority means nothing more than "freedom, autonomy, and strength." These virtues look surprisingly like those of the phallic pen to which Gilbert and Gubar, asking "with what organ can females generate texts?" seek a feminist alternative. Moreover, despite the acuity of their individual analyses, Gilbert and Gubar force themselves into the peculiar position of implying that authorship—a role superior to that of the "mere character"—involves a redemption from "literacy," that the ideal author is somehow external to her text, beyond or above textuality. Significantly, this attitude places them in the unlikely company of certain

---

From *PMLA* 100, no. 5 (October 1985).

male critics whose mistrust of "literacy," or literariness, derives from an ideology with which feminism would seem to have little in common.

In an almost canonical gesture, critics of *Emma* stigmatize linguistic playfulness, or merely a fondness for the written word, as a threat to moral well-being. Marvin Mudrick typifies this stance, indicting in both the novel and its heroine—"whom," Austen predicted, "no one but myself will much like"—what he calls the "triumph of surface," where the scandal of "wit adrift from feeling" finds its objective correlative in Emma's latent lesbianism. Admittedly, Gilbert and Gubar differ from Austen's male critics in their reasons for wanting to separate self and text. Whereas the latter equate literariness with frivolity and narcissism, the former view it as an effect of living in the "tight place" to which women are condemned. Pushed dangerously close to the contaminating world of signs, the Austenian heroine, like Austen herself, must exercise extraordinary ingenuity to keep her autonomous selfhood intact. Both the feminist critics and the conservatives, however, despite their manifest political differences, subscribe to the ideology of character implicit in Malcolm Bradbury's observation that *Emma* persuades us "to see the full human being as full, fine, morally serious, totally responsible, entirely involved, and to consider every human action as a crucial committing act of self-definition."

As D. A. Miller has noted, Austen's quiet authority tends to intimidate even her shrewdest readers. Yet when characters in her work suggest not the plenitude invoked by Bradbury but, rather, the artifice and materiality of *written* characters, moralism encounters significant obstacles. To locate these linguistic residues, these scandals of "literacy," is to identify traces of Austen's own rebellion against an overly reassuring moral ideology, traces that intimate a subversiveness far more interesting than that imagined by Gilbert and Gubar.

A brief passage from *Mansfield Park* (1814) will serve as a prelude to the tensions at work in *Emma* (1816) and as proof that, even in what looks like her most authoritarian novel, Austen can disrupt her own orthodoxy. The description concerns Fanny Price's attempt, late in the novel, to introduce her sister to the pleasures of reading:

> after a few days, the remembrance of her books grew so potent and stimulative, that Fanny found it impossible not to try for books again. There were none in her father's house; but wealth is luxurious and daring—and some of hers found its way to a circulating library. She became a subscriber—amazed at being

> any thing *in propria persona*, amazed at her own doings in every way; to be a renter, a chuser of books! And to be having any one's improvement in view of her choice! But so it was. Susan had read nothing, and Fanny longed to give her a share in her own first pleasures, and inspire a taste for the biography and poetry which she delighted in herself.

The exultant tone of Austen's *style indirect libre* imitates Fanny's joy on realizing herself as what Bradbury calls a "full human being." Yet the giddiness of the passage may also betoken Austen's response to an inconspicuous but "potent and stimulative" contradiction. For the embarrassing fact that the passage just barely conceals is that Fanny comes into her own only by entering a system of exchange, a circulating library. To be "any thing *in propria persona*," Fanny must spend her wealth, dispersing it into a larger economy; to consolidate her personhood, she has to insert herself into a constantly fluctuating literary structure. It is precisely her fall into "literacy," or literariness, that establishes Fanny's selfhood.

This passage merits attention not because it speaks of reading and writing: these themes occur often enough—and often innocently—in Austen's novels. Its interest, rather, lies in the way its literary references hint at some more than merely thematic literariness, some nagging but unspecifiable linguistic opacity in the novel itself. By collapsing the distance, moreover, between self and text—between a saving inwardness and a dangerously verbal sociability—the passage confounds categories that the novel posits elsewhere as opposites.

In *Emma*, this unsettling of polarities finds its wittiest advocate in the heroine herself, who, in a characteristic move, complains that Mr. Knightley, the novel's "normative and exemplary figure," finds their respective judgments "not near enough to give me a chance of being right, if we think differently." Yet Emma's attempt to substitute difference for opposition is more than just a clever piece of sophistry. Emma is frequently "wrong," as she is here, but perhaps she is "right" to question the absoluteness with which Knightley does in fact view the distinction between them. Perhaps, moreover, her "wrongness" is often closer to being "right"—that is, to yielding knowledge of the fictions that sustain social existence—than Knightley and his scholarly advocates will admit. Patriarchal criticism of *Emma*, of course, takes Knightley's side, portraying the narrative as a conflict in which "right" seeks to appropriate "wrong" and to recast it (her) in its (his) own image. It is possible, however, to pursue an apparently perverse but more critically productive tactic: we can give Emma some respect and construe the conflict dialectically, treating it less as an opposition and more as a difference.

We might try, then, to read the novel as a contest between Emma and Knightley, a contest between two equally compelling interpretations of the self—especially the female self—and society. Knightley states his views succinctly when he objects to Emma's adoption of Harriet Smith as her protégée: "I am much mistaken if Emma's doctrines give any strength of mind, or tend at all to make a girl adapt herself rationally to the varieties of her situation in life.—They only give a little polish." Despite the stark opposition that Knightley's terms suggest, the difference between the two implicit pedagogies cannot be simplified as the difference between a serious and a playful education or between a moral and an aesthetic one. For if Knightley's "strength of mind" borders on the conformist virtue of "adaptability," Emma's "polish," while it signals a politics of superficiality, is by no means superficial.

Whenever characters in *Emma* seem merely to be playing with words, the stakes are in fact much higher. One particularly instructive episode revolves around "puzzles," anagrams that the contestants must unscramble. Here the chief competitors are not Knightley and Emma but Knightley and Frank Churchill, whose recalcitrance, as we will see, Emma refines. Knightley dislikes Frank Churchill, not only because the younger man seems to be a rival for Emma's affections but also because Frank presumes to "read every body's character." Having just let slip a possible clue to his involvement with Jane Fairfax, and regretting his carelessness, Frank uses the word game as a pretext for apology:

> Frank Churchill placed a word before Miss Fairfax. She gave a slight glance around the table, and applied herself to it. Frank was next to Emma, Jane opposite to them—and Mr. Knightley so placed as to see them all; and it was his object to see as much as he could, with as little apparent observation. The word was discovered, and with a faint smile pushed away.

As Knightley's stance here shows, his resentment of Frank stems in part from his fear that Frank may usurp the role of master reader: it is Knightley alone who shall reserve the right "to read every body's character," to be "so placed as to see them all." Knightley's motives here are typical: if *Emma*, as many critics have noted, is a detective novel, then Knightley, even more than Emma herself, aspires to the role of chief detective. For while Emma is content to fantasize about various romantic scenarios involving Frank Churchill, Knightley will not rest until he has seen into the heart of the mystery surrounding Frank and Jane. For Knightley, reading fosters "strength of mind," but it is also a mode of surveillance.

By acting *un*interested, Knightley would appear *dis*interested as well. But his surreptitious behavior undermines the notion of disinterested reading. Seeing without appearing to observe, reading without appearing to read, Knightley at once admits and suppresses this duplicity. Later in the novel, the fervor with which he praises the "disinterestedness" of Jane's love for Frank, when in fact her own pecuniary and perhaps erotic interest in that relationship seems considerable, betrays Knightley's extraordinary interest in disinterestedness, a virtue he is apt to see even where it does not exist. Earlier in the novel, the vehemence with which he denounces Frank, whom he does not even know yet, strikes Emma as "unworthy the real liberality of mind which she was always used to acknowledge in him." Of course, the most memorable illustration of Knightley's partiality is his comically nitpicking reading of Frank's long letter to Mrs. Weston, a reading whose reductiveness Emma labors to mitigate. However "impressive and admirable" Knightley may be, he is hardly an innocent interpreter.

Knightley continues his detective work, recalling the incriminating remark that Frank has tried to explain away by recourse to an alleged "dream":

> The word was *blunder*; and as Harriet exultingly proclaimed it, there was a blush on Jane's cheek which gave it a meaning not otherwise ostensible. Mr. Knightley connected it with the dream; but how it could all be, was beyond his comprehension. How the delicacy, the discretion of his favourite could have been so lain asleep! He feared there must be some decided involvement. Disingenuousness and double-dealing seemed to meet him at every turn. These letters were but the vehicle for gallantry and trick. It was a child's play, chosen to conceal a deeper game on Frank Churchill's part.

Joseph Wiesenfarth observes that the "word 'blunder' runs like a discord through the novel, indicating mistakes that are made in the games of words as well as in the more serious and dangerous games of matchmaking." The recurrence of the word points indeed to the centrality of misinterpretation and misbehavior in this would-be bildungsroman. Yet the problems that a proper education—or at least one overseen by

Knightley—would correct may be more fundamental than mere "mistakes": the discord that runs through the novel may signify a certain perverse malfunctioning that can be neither corrected nor even regulated. For what disturbs Knightley here is that his attempts at interpretive mastery of Frank Churchill's game meet with resistance; he encounters not just the temporary unintelligibility of scrambled letters but the much greater recalcitrance of "disingenuousness and double-dealing." As we have seen, Knightley's own posture partakes of a certain disingenuousness as well. Yet he cannot accept Frank's "puzzles" as more than just structurally puzzling. What should have been mere "child's play" has turned out "to conceal a deeper game," and Knightley can tolerate only a socially sanctioned and therefore superficial "depth," only a legible illegibility. The social mechanism favored by Knightley contains and neutralizes subjectivity by encoding it within a cultural alphabet, so that one may read character by reading the characters, or letters, that a character forms.

The first sign of malfunctioning appears when Jane's blush gives the word *blunder* a "meaning," but one "not otherwise ostensible." Thus finding the affair "beyond his comprehension," Knightley experiences the same blockage that awaits the reader who approaches Jane Austen's novels unprepared for their frequent literariness, expecting only the easeful wisdom of "gentle Jane." Frank's "deeper game" defies Knightley's authority, refusing to confirm the older man as the paternal or patriarchal supervisor of children at play. For such, in Knightley's view, is the purpose of games. Since they presuppose rules, they emblematize the governability of society. To the extent that they include a moment of limited opacity, games permit the illusion that each player's individual self possesses a unique interiority. To the extent that they subordinate this individuality to an ultimately decipherable code, games ensure the transparency of the self. The real winner, thus, is the ideology of institutional control—or what Knightley will refer to euphemistically as the "beauty of truth and sincerity in all our dealings with each other."

At least in this round, however, that ideology loses: the most that Knightley can infer is "some decided involvement," probably of Frank Churchill with Jane Fairfax. Frank would appear triumphant for the time being despite his blunder, because he has rewritten the rules of the game so that the game itself is no longer the same. To assume, as Knightley does, that "these letters were but the vehicle for gallantry and trick" is not to understand the new game but, rather, to concede its mystery.

Vehicles and conveyance loom large in the next problematic passage as well. In one of her rare utterances, the shadowy Jane Fairfax, talking with Knightley's brother, delivers a surprisingly impassioned hymn to the postal service:

> "The post office is a wonderful establishment!" said she.—"The regularity and dispatch of it! If one thinks of all that it has to do, and all that it does so well, it is really astonishing!"
>
> "It is certainly very well regulated."
>
> "So seldom that any negligence or blunder appears! So seldom that a letter, among the thousands that are constantly passing about the kingdom, is even carried wrong—and not one in a million, I supppose, actually lost! And when one considers the variety of hands, and of bad hands too, that are to be deciphered, it increases the wonder!"

Certain "literary" institutions seem to inspire a significant rhetorical excess in Austen's novels: Jane's praise of the post office is as suspiciously feverish as Fanny's delight in belonging to the library. Offering her own version of the Lacanian dictum that "a letter always arrives at its destination," Jane may very well be denying her fear that letters do not always arrive where and when they should. If Lacan's formulation insists on the inevitability of a certain system or structure, then Jane's hyperbolic encomium both represses and reveals grave doubts about the inevitability of any system or structure whatsoever. We will learn, of course, that Jane is concerned about the "regularity" of her clandestine correspondence with Frank Churchill and that, indeed, their engagement is broken off as a result of a serious blunder on the part not of the post office but of Frank himelf: he simply forgets to mail an all-important letter. Yet the postal service is merely a synecdoche for the much larger system of communication on which the novel centers—namely, the social text in which the characters keep construing and misconstruing one another—so that any anxiety about mail deliveries may be taken as an anxiety about the semiotic efficiency or governability of society as a whole.

Jane's desire, then, that blunders never appear—her need to assert that of all the letters "constantly passing about the kingdom . . . not one in a million [is] actually lost"—originates in the same ideology as does Knightley's impatience with Frank's "deeper game." Bad handwritten is to Jane what "disinterestedness and double-dealing" are to Knightley: both complicate the operation of "deciphering," compromising any institution that would call itself "very well regulated." Yet Jane has said not that blunders never appear, only that they "seldom" appear. Even she can acknowledge the possibility of handwriting so bad, so shamefully illegible, that no strategy of deciphering could contain it. Should it "spread," such handwriting could eventually disrupt the entire system of coding and decoding, of writing and reading—in short, of communication—by which a Mr. Knightley might define society.

But what would such handwriting look like? Insofar as it resisted deciphering, it might be too cipher-bound to admit of interpretation. What would it mean, though, to be cipher-bound, or even to be a cipher? Paraphrasing a poem by Anne Finch, Gilbert and Gubar write: "*all* females are 'Cyphers'—nullities, vacancies—existing merely and punningly to increase male 'Numbers' (either poems or persons) by pleasuring either men's bodies or their minds, their penises or their pens." Bad or excessively "ciphered" handwriting would thus represent a sort of *degré zéro de l'écriture*, writing so "ladylike" in its vacuousness that it would refuse to add up to anything like a meaning. It is tempting to view the devaluation of women as ending up ironically subverting patriarchal arithmetic. Yet just how would that subversion come about? For answers, we might turn again to *Mansfield Park*, whose heroine, as Leo Bersani points out, "almost is *not*." Fanny's aunt, Lady Bertram, may come even closer to the condition of nothingness: one of the other characters refers to her as "more of a cipher now" than when her husband, away on business, is at home. That phrase typifies the sarcasm that Austen reserves for particularly insipid characters, but it also suggests something more interesting. For how can anyone be more—or less—of a cipher? Either one is a cipher or one is not. In replacing a definition of the cipher as a mere zero with an understanding of ciphers as quantities susceptible of increase and decrease, Austen reminds us of the radical instability of the term. For ciphers are not just numbers but figures as well, and the word *cipher* itself imitates the shiftiness of verbal figures. Just as figures of speech mean something other than themselves, so ciphers are figures both in the mathematical sense and in the more elusive rhetorical sense: "symbolic characters," according to *Webster's New International Dictionary*, ciphers are letters as well as numbers, but letters that call their own literality into question. No longer mere zeros, ciphers designate that species of "bad handwriting" known as figurative language, which, by exceeding the literal, may prevent letters from arriving at their destinations. Figurative language marks the blundering that threatens the orderly delivery of messages.

One such subversive slippage from mathematical exactness to

rhetorical uncertainty takes up almost all of chapter 9 in the first volume of *Emma*, a chapter that has to do precisely with ciphers. We have seen Knightley criticize Emma's educational principles because "They only give a little polish," but here we observe the decisive role of ciphers in transforming the curriculum of a finishing school into a politics of superficiality. A moralistic reading will assume that the chapter—not to mention the novel as a whole—has been written from the viewpoint of Mr. Knightley, the "custodian of Jane Austen's judgment." But a reading more sensitive to Austen's figures will discover elements that evade such deciphering. In the following passage, which describes the academic program Emma has devised for Harriet, we may discern both authoritarian and subversive discourses:

> Her views of improving her little friend's mind, by a great deal of useful reading and conversation, had never yet led to more than a few first chapters, and the intention of going on tomorrow. It was much easier to chat than to study; much pleasanter to let her imagination range and work at Harriet's fortune, than to be labouring to enlarge her comprehension or exercise it on sober facts; and the only literary pursuit which engaged Harriet at present, the only mental provision she was making for the evening of life, was the collecting and transcribing all the riddles of every sort that she could meet with, into a thin quarto of hot-pressed paper, made up by her friend, and ornamented with cyphers and trophies.

Knightley has already mentioned Emma's long-standing propensity for drawing up lists of books to read, only to abandon her ambitious plans. "I have done with expecting any course of steady reading from Emma," he announces, explaining that "she will never submit to any thing requiring industry and patience, and a subjection of the fancy to the understanding." In acknowledging that Emma and Harriet can never get beyond "a few first chapters," this later passage seems to confirm his opinion. It supports the numerous interpretations of *Emma* as a negative portrait of the artist, as an exorcism of the "imaginist" or solipsist in Austen herself. Indeed, the gently mocking description of Harriet's sole "literary pursuit" seems, more seriously, to indict Emma, who would rather "let her imagination range and work at Harriet's fortune," enmeshing her in flimsy little novels of sensibility, than develop in both her pupil and herself enough *Sitzfleisch* to follow her ambitious syllabus.

Emma is, admittedly, acting like a bad novelist. Yet the "badness" of her "novels" corresponds less to the immaturity and capriciousness of one who has not read enough than to the semiotic aberrance of someone with "bad handwriting." For though Emma's curriculum may not involve much reading, she and Harriet spend a great deal of time writing—specifically, "collecting and transcribing all the riddles of every sort that [Harriet] could meet with, into a thin quarto of hot-pressed paper, made up by her friend, and ornamented with cyphers and trophies." Here, of course, Knightley could find all the evidence he needs to convict Emma of pedagogical malpractice: not only does the copying of riddles seem like a stultifying waste of time; the very cover of the riddle book emblematizes the meaninglessness of mere decoration. But, as we have suggested, while "cyphers" may escape the stratagems of meaning, they are hardly without significance. We might remember Austen's "merely" ornamental analogy for her own art—a "little bit (two Inches wide) of Ivory." Interestingly enough, the "cyphers" on Harriet's riddle book exist alongside "trophies," pictures of prizes. Trophies imply victory—which in turn implies conflict—and relate etymologically to tropes. As we will see, this chapter stages a battle between figurative language and figuring out, between ciphers and deciphering, between Emma's deep superficiality and Knightley's superficial depth.

"Depth," here, signifies subversive complexity, not just "strength of mind," which, as Knightley intimates, presupposes the ability to "submit and "subject" oneself. Yet if the ciphers on the cover of the riddle book suggest the first kind of depth, they do so otherwise than by pointing to a plot below—and more politically serious than—what Gilbert and Gubar call "Jane Austen's Cover Story." For ciphers, as the dictionary reminds us, can be "texts in secret writing," monograms of some systematically dissimulated referent—in short, riddles. Here one *can* judge a book by its cover: the ciphers on the cover of Harriet's book cover the ciphers inside, which turn out to represent not ultimate truth but merely more covering.

Now, such a conception of the relation between surface and depth may seem less than subversive. In fact, it might appear entirely compatible with Knightley's belief that because games permit illusions of depth they guarantee—in their function as "child's play"—patriarchal control. How is it, then, that ciphers serve the antiauthoritarian cause? How, in Emma's hands, do they become figures of disruption? How does the play of surfaces in which they are implicated become deep in the subversive sense, rather than in either the authoritarian sense or even the sense that Gilbert and Gubar's notion of a feminist subtext might imply? If the chapter supports authoritarian as well as subversive readings and at the same time dramatizes the conflict between them, that conflict is not between figurative language and literal language but between two interpretations of figurative language. Where the "Knightleian" interpretation grounds figurative language in social rules, the "Emmaesque" interpretation sees it as inherently ungroundable, even in any politically acceptable subtext. Although Knightley himself does not appear in the chapter, we may identify as his proxy the eligible young bachelor Mr. Elton, whom Emma is busy imagining as Harriet's suitor and whose amorous riddle supplies Emma with an irresistible opportunity for creative misreading. Let us look at the pre-text out of which she constructs one of her best "bad novels":

To Miss ______.

CHARADE.

My first displays the wealth and pomp of kings,
Lords of the earth! their luxury and ease.
Another view of man, my second brings,
Behold him there, the monarch of the seas!

But, ah! united, what reverse we have!
Man's boasted power and freedom, all are flown;
Lord of the earth and sea, he bends a slave,
And woman, lovely woman, reigns alone.

Thy ready wit the word will soon supply,
May its approval beam in that soft eye!

The misreading begins even before Emma reads the charade, as soon as she tells Harriet: "Take it, it is for you. Take your own." Ownership is indeed at issue both in the interpretation of this riddle and in the novel as a whole, and in failing to see herself as the rightful "owner" of Elton's riddle, Emma is at odds with the novel's ethic of property and propriety. The riddle itself is profoundly concerned with "wealth and pomp," "power and freedom." Announcing his interest in "courtship," Elton at the same time, as Paul H. Fry cogently notes, betrays a preoccupation with "Power (court) and Wealth (naval commerce) . . . that prove[s] to the unblindered eye that [he] will never marry Harriet Smith." A reading less willful than Emma's would, of course, have paid more attention to the way in which Elton's characters express his character. Yet to be at once a reading and a writing—to exemplify productive error— Emma's reading has to be not only a reading of emblems but also an emblem in its own right. In a sense, Emma reads the riddle all too well. For if Elton's flattering rhetoric hints conventionally at a "reverse" of conventional power structures, Emma's misreading enacts that very "reverse," reading his figures unconventionally.

Offering an alternative to the patriarchal view of reading as a regimen for "strengthening the mind" and forming character, Emma's misreading arises from a radically different understanding of character. Whereas the patriarchal program would form character by inserting the self into the slots of convention, the subversive counterprogram begins by defining the self as a slot. On the one hand, Elton's caption, "To Miss ______," merely indicates that the whole business of courtship is a sort of prefabricated "text," a series of conventional performances: if the offering of flirtatious riddles is the first stage of the game, then the rules require that the young riddler honor the modesty topos by leaving the young woman's name blank, as in some contemporary novel, and that she, moreover, regard herself as playing a game, acting a part in a ready-made fiction. According to this view, one forms one's character by recognizing one's status as character in a novel not of one's own design. On the other hand, "To Miss ______" could be rewritten figuratively as "To Miss Blank." Not only does this rewriting magnify the conventionality—we might even say the "emptiness"—of Elton's formula, but it also invokes the very sign of emptiness or lack on which the subversive discourse turns. For a blank is a kind of zero or cipher. Yet if a cipher is not just a zero but a sign of figurality as well, then "To Miss Blank" conjoins femininity itself with the disruptive irregularity of figurative language. From a patriarchal perspective, woman is a zero waiting to fill a blank space; from a subversive perspective, "Miss Cipher" is the name for the irreducible figurality of the self, whether male or female.

Emma's misreading, then, produces a "novel" in "bad handwriting," a "novel" whose female characters personify this illegibility. Such a reading, however, neither proclaims the "enigma of woman" nor ascribes to women the power of self-authoring. To appreciate its full force—to know what the association of women with ciphers involves—we must find out why Emma fills the blank with Harriet's name rather than her own. Why, after she has subjected the riddle to a thorough analysis, does Emma persist in the delusion that it was intended for Harriet? How, in getting part of the riddle "wrong," does Emma produce an interpretation that is curiously "right"? If the conventional view of character insists that one accept one's place in a predetermined social text, then the subversive view of the self as a rhetorical figure—not just as a figure or character in a novel—can be charged with narcissistic implications: to see oneself as a trope may be to revel in aesthetic self-admiration. And indeed, precisely this charge has been leveled against Emma. Darrel Mansell, for example, writes that Harriet "never amounts to much more than a projection of Emma's own personality onto a blank, reflecting surface." Though Harriet does belong to that group of Austenian characters who, as Leo Bersani would say, almost are not, the mere fact of her blankness does not render Emma's relationship with her narcissistic. Something more complex than narcissism characterizes this relationship. For in misreading "Miss ______," Emma at once puts Harriet where she herself should be and assumes Harriet's place. Filling the blank with "Smith" instead of "Woodhouse," Emma not only cedes her slot to Harriet but also installs herself in Harriet's habitual position—that of blankness.

The Emma described as "clever" in the first sentence of the novel thus discloses an element of Harriet in herself. It is almost as if, for a moment, Emma and Harriet had become a composite character, so that Emma's assumption that the riddle was intended for Harriet seems oddly appropriate. We might say that the difference between a rhetorical figure and a figure in a novel is the difference between composite and unitary characters, except that to define the self as a rhetorical figure is to suggest the compositeness—the overdetermination—of all characters. As characters in a novel, Harriet and Emma fall short of uniqueness and unity because, substituting for each other, they "mean" something other than themselves, just as a rhetorical figure means something other than itself. Even Elton's riddle supports this theory of the overdetermined self, since its closing couplet speaks of the loved one's "ready wit," clearly an Emma-like attribute, and of her "soft eye," which, Emma says, is "Harriet exactly." Now, the incompatibility of these epithets may signal the insincerity, or merely the inaccuracy, that results from "going by the book," as Elton has done. Later, when Emma has learned Elton's true intentions, she corroborates this view, musing indignantly, "To be sure, the charade, with its 'ready wit'—but then, the 'soft eyes'—in fact it suited neither; it was a jumble without taste or truth." Repentant, she seems to disavow her first reading. Yet even in this implicit concession to Knightley—even as she repudiates her "novel"—Emma articulates the most subversive insight of her misreading. For what that misreading discovers is that the real "jumble" is not so much the riddle as the self. Now she blames Elton's want of taste for the very fascination that underlies her relationship with Harriet—a fascination not with the self but with the otherness of the self, with the heterogeneity that Emma-as-Harriet and Harriet-as-Emma embody. No wonder Emma realizes "that Mr. Knightley must marry no one but herself" only after Harriet has confessed *her* love for Knightley: Harriet's discourse is the discourse of the other, the other lodged within Emma herself.

Occupied by rival ideologies, chapter 9 typifies the ambiguity that unsettles the narrative at several junctures. Read from Knightley's point of view, the chapter demonstrates what can happen without a "subjection of the fancy to the understanding." Read from Emma's point of view, it allegorizes a theory of the self that rejects the hierarchical terms of the first ideology, organizing the self horizontally and contingently rather than vertically and paradigmatically. Moreover, although the Emma-Elton-Harriet imbroglio is exposed fairly early in the novel, the misreading performed in chapter 9 anticipates other setbacks in what looks like Knightley's gradual conquest of Emma. One such instance occurs during the famous excursion to Box Hill, in the course of which Emma insults Miss Bates. There, the politics of superficiality presents itself once again in the form of characters and word games. Amid the general unpleasantness of the outing, Mr. Weston offers a conundrum, asking the party, "What two letters of the alphabet are there, that express perfection?" The answer is "M. and A.—Em-Ma," and "Emma found a great deal to laugh at and enjoy in it." Knightley, however, takes the conundrum as an opportunity to reprove Emma, saying "*Perfection* should not have come quite so soon." With characteristic moral seriousness, he reads the characters to read Emma's character, finding in what Austen calls a "very indifferent piece of wit" an image for that character's imperfection or incompletion. Two letters have been left out of Emma's name, and Knightley wishes to see Emma's character made whole. Yet the badness of the pun partakes also of the "badness" we have come to associate with figurative language, and it is precisely this "badness" that Emma "enjoys." For Mr. Weston has reminded her that character need not be a homogeneous entity, that it is an aggregate of many different characters, that the self is no more a fixed identity than the name, a construct susceptible to fragmentation and rearrangement.

In recalling the otherness of the self, moreover, Emma sees herself through otherness, as another sees her. What Knightley would chastise as narcissistic self-absorption is in fact an acknowledgment that one is embedded in a "text" more intricate than one's own name. If Knightley conceives the social text as conferring on the self a predetermined—hence illusory—subjectivity, Emma's social text figures collective existence as an endless collaborative process of reading and writing, in which the self emerges as a site of overlapping interpretations. Emma's valetudinarian father writes melodramatic letters about her misadventure with the gypsies, for "if he did not invent illnesses for her, she could make no figure in a message." The social text that Emma inhabits comprises any number of such "inventions": like everyone else in this world, she is always "making a figure" in one message or another, because she is always being reinvented, or reread, both by herself and by other selves.

Even marriage—the apotheosis of the "beauty of truth and sincerity in all our dealings with each other," the paradigm of "every thing that is decided and open"—is marked by the fictiveness and the evasions of the social. For despite Knightley's declaration that he and Emma have finally arrived at a state of mutual transparency, at the end of the novel she is still practicing "disguise, equivocation [and] mystery" in not revealing that Harriet is in love with him. As [Marvin] Mudrick observes, "There is no happy ending"—at least not if happiness lies in the ideal of society as an ultimately legible text composed of and by a homogeneous set of interpretive conventions. The novel ends instead with a trio of marriages whose unintelligibility, not only to outsiders but perhaps even to the partners themselves, suggests a densely woven fabric of fictions and misreadings.

Oddly enough, it is Knightley, of all people, who contemplates the need for both fictionality and error. Late in the novel, on one of the few occasions when he praises Emma unreservedly, he also pays the highest compliment to the subversive theory of the self:

> My interference was quite as likely to do harm as good. It was very natural for you to say, what right has he to lecture me?—and I am afraid very natural for you to feel that it was done in a disagreeable manner. I do not believe I did you any good. The good was all to myself, by making you an object of the tenderest affection to me. I could not think about you so much without doating on you, faults and all; and by dint of fancying so many errors, have been in love with you ever since you were thirteen at least.

Is this speech merely a display of gallantry on the part of a conqueror whose defeated adversary has shown sufficient signs of humility? While it is possible to dismiss these remarks as Emma's reward for submitting, the last sentence in particular has a concessive force that puts it beyond the less-than-sincere rhetoric of the gracious winner. Knightley, after all, is telling Emma not just that he loves her, "faults and all," but that he himself has "fancied" or invented "many" of those "errors." If the narrative has traditionally been conceived as a linear development whereby Emma, changing under Knightley's influence, moves gradually toward a welcoming recognition of that influence, now the Pygmalion myth gets a new twist: Knightley is interested less in perfecting the "object of [his] tenderest affection" than in "fancying"—at once imagining and liking—her charming imperfections. The dissatisfaction Knightley voices when he criticizes Mr. Weston's feeble conundrum thus appears in a different light: "*Perfection* should not have come quite so soon" no longer means "Unfortunately, Emma is not yet perfect"; it might be glossed more accurately as "Thank you, Mr. Weston, but I wish to continue enjoying Emma's imperfections for a while." Demanding perfection so that he may invent further imperfections, denouncing Emma's errors so that he may fancy more of them, Knightley in fact desires nothing less than an indefinite postponement of that conquest toward which he seems to aspire.

Instead of resolving itself into a linear progression, then, the narrative turns out to be going in circles. Those who bemoan the absence of a "happy ending"—of more persuasive proof that Emma has been converted—are impatient with precisely this circularity. For the failure of the linear model implies a failure of the unilateral ethical scheme in which a morally superior Knightley transforms a morally inferior Emma. Whereas it was his job to rescue her from literariness and its attendant ethical dangers, now he too appears to be tangled up in that net. Pretending to "sober and direct" her, he has ended up egging her on to further bouts of misguided fiction making. Knightley's words suggest how complicated the picture has become: "fancying so many errors," he is no more a mere critic than Emma is a mere fiction maker. His interpretations are flights of fancy, which she must read to produce her little novels of error, to which he in turn takes a fancy, producing additional fanciful interpretations. Austen is at her most subversive, then, not in intimating the antisocial recesses of her heroine's interiority but in locating Emma in this potentially endless circuit of fiction, interpretation, and desire, with its dynamic and reciprocal relations between men and women. When the self is an effect of its overdetermined acts and society is not one text but a continuously revolving or circulating library, the descent into literacy becomes a fortunate fall.

Chronology

1775 Jane Austen is born on December 16 in the village of Steventon, Hampshire, to George Austen, parish clergyman, and Cassandra Leigh Austen. She is the seventh of eight children. She and her sister Cassandra are educated at Oxford and Southampton by the widow of a Principal of Brasenose College, and then attend the Abbey School at Reading. Jane's formal education ends when she is nine years old.

1787–93 Austen writes various pieces for the amusement of her family (now collected in the three volumes of *Juvenilia*), the most famous of which is *Love and Freindship*. She and her family also perform in the family barn various plays and farces, some of which are written by Jane.

1793–95 Austen writes her first novel, the epistolary *Lady Susan*, and begins the epistolary *Elinor and Marianne*, which will become *Sense and Sensibility*.

1796–97 Austen completes *First Impressions*, an early version of *Pride and Prejudice*. Her father tries to get it published without success. Austen begins *Sense and Sensibility* and *Northanger Abbey*.

1798 Austen finishes a version of *Northanger Abbey*.

1801 George Austen retires to Bath with his family.

1801–2 Jane Austen probably suffers from an unhappy love affair (the man in question is believed to have died suddenly), and also probably becomes engaged for a day to Harris Bigg-Wither.

1803 Austen sells a two-volume manuscript entitled *Susan* to a publisher for £10. It is advertised, but never printed. This is a version of *Northanger Abbey*, probably later revised.

1803–5 Austen writes ten chapters of *The Watsons*, which is never finished.

1805 George Austen dies. Jane abandons work on *The Watsons*.

1805–6 Jane Austen, her mother, and her sister live in various lodgings in Bath.

1806–9 The three Austen women move to Southampton, living near one of Jane's brothers.

1809 The three Austen women move to Chawton Cottage, in Hampshire, which is part of the estate of Jane's brother Edward Austen (later Knight), who has been adopted by Thomas Knight, a relative. Edward has just lost his wife, who died giving birth to her tenth child, and the household has been taken over by Jane's favorite niece, Fanny.

1811 Austen decides to publish *Sense and Sensibility* at her own expense, and anonymously. It comes out in November, in three volumes.

1811–12 Austen is probably revising *First Impressions* extensively and beginning *Mansfield Park*.

1813 *Pride and Prejudice: A Novel. In Three Volumes. By the Author of "Sense and Sensibility"* is published in January. Second editions of both books come out in November.

1814 *Mansfield Park* is published, again anonymously and in three volumes. It sells out by November. Austen begins *Emma*.

1815 Austen finishes *Emma* and begins *Persuasion*. *Emma* is published in December, anonymously, in three volumes, by a new publisher.

1816 A second edition of *Mansfield Park* is published.

1817 A third edition of *Pride and Prejudice* is published. Austen begins *Sanditon*. She moves to Winchester, where she dies, after a year-long illness, on July 18. She is buried in Winchester Cathedral. After her death, her family destroys much of her correspondence in order to protect her reputation.

1818 *Persuasion* and *Northanger Abbey* are published posthumously together, their authorship still officially anonymous.

Contributors

HAROLD BLOOM, Sterling Professor of the Humanities at Yale University, is the author of *The Anxiety of Influence, Poetry and Repression,* and many other volumes of literary criticism. His forthcoming study, *Freud: Transference and Authority*, attempts a full-scale reading of all of Freud's major writings. A MacArthur Prize Fellow, he is general editor of five series of literary criticism published by Chelsea House.

STUART M. TAVE is William Rainey Harper Professor in the College and Professor of English at the University of Chicago. His books include *Some Words of Jane Austen, New Essays by De Quincey*, and a study of comic theory and criticism in the eighteenth and nineteenth centuries.

JOHN HAGAN teaches at the State University of New York, Binghamton.

JULIET MCMASTER is Professor of English at the University of Alberta. She is the author of *Thackeray: The Major Novels, Trollope's Palliser Novels: Theme and Pattern,* and *Jane Austen on Love.*

JULIA PREWITT BROWN is the author of *Jane Austen's Novels: Social Change and Literary Form.*

SUSAN MORGAN is Assistant Professor of English at Stanford University and the author of *In the Meantime: Character and Perception in Jane Austen's Fiction*.

JOHN PETER RUMRICH is Assistant Professor of English at Fordham University, the Bronx. He has written on the *Faerie Queene* and *Paradise Lost.*

JAN FERGUS is Assistant Professor of English at Lehigh University and the author of *Jane Austen and the Didactic Novel.*

Patricia Meyer Spacks is Professor of English and Chairman of the Department at Yale University. Her books include *The Female Imagination* and *Gossip*.

Joseph Litvak is Assistant Professor of English at Bowdoin College.

Bibliography

Babb, Howard. *Jane Austen's Novels: The Fabric of Dialogue*. Columbus: Ohio State University Press, 1962.

Berger, Carole. "The Rake and the Reader in Jane Austen's Novels." *Studies in English Literature 1500–1900* 15 (1975): 531–44.

Bloom, Harold, ed. *Modern Critical Views: Jane Austen*. New Haven: Chelsea House, 1986.

Boles, Carolyn G. "Jane Austen and the Reader: Rhetorical Techniques in *Northanger Abbey, Pride and Prejudice,* and *Emma*." *Emporia State Research Studies* 30, no. 1 (1981): 152–67.

Bowen, Elizabeth. "Jane Austen." In *The English Novelists*, edited by Derek Verschoyle, 101–13. New York: Harcourt, Brace, 1936.

Bradbrook, Frank. *Jane Austen and Her Predecessors*. Cambridge: Cambridge University Press, 1967.

Brown, Lloyd. *Bits of Ivory: Narrative Techniques in Jane Austen's Fiction*. Baton Rouge: Louisiana State University Press, 1973.

Bush, Douglas. *Jane Austen*. New York: Macmillan, 1975.

Butler, Marilyn. *Jane Austen and the War of Ideas*. Oxford: Oxford University Press, 1975.

Cecil, David. *A Portrait of Jane Austen*. New York: Hill & Wang, 1980.

Chabot, C. Barry. "Jane Austen's Novels: The Vicissitudes of Desire." *American Imago* 32 (1975): 288–308.

Chapman, R. W. *Jane Austen: Facts and Problems*. Oxford: Clarendon Press, 1948.

Colby, R. A. *Fiction with a Purpose*. Bloomington: Indiana University Press, 1967.

Craik, W. A. *Jane Austen: The Six Novels*. London: Methuen, 1966.

DeRose, Peter. "Marriage and Self-Knowledge in *Emma* and *Pride and Prejudice*." *Renascence* 30 (1978): 199–216.

Devlin, David. *Jane Austen and Education*. New York: Barnes & Noble, 1975.

Donovan, Robert. *The Shaping Vision: Imagination in the English Novel from Defoe to Dickens*. Ithaca: Cornell University Press, 1966.

Duckworth, Alistair. *The Improvement of the Estate: A Study of Jane Austen's Novels*. Baltimore: The Johns Hopkins University Press, 1971.

Edge, Charles. "*Emma:* A Technique of Characterization." In *The Classic British Novel*, edited by Howard M. Harper, Jr., and Charles Edge, 51–64. Athens: University of Georgia Press, 1972.

Frazer, June M. "Stylistic Categories of Narrative in Jane Austen." *Style* 17, no. 1 (1983): 16–26.

Fry, Paul H. "Georgic Comedy: The Fictive Territory of Jane Austen's *Emma*." *Studies in the Novel* 11, no. 2 (1979): 129–46.

Gilbert, Sandra M., and Susan Gubar. *The Madwoman in the Attic: The Woman Writer and the Nineteenth-Century Literary Imagination*. New Haven: Yale University Press, 1979.

Gillie, Christopher. *A Preface to Jane Austen*. London: Longmans, Green, 1975.

Halperin, John. *The Life of Jane Austen*. Sussex: Harvester Press, 1984.

———, ed. *Jane Austen: Bicentenary Essays*. Cambridge: Cambridge University Press, 1975.

Hardy, Barbara. *A Reading of Jane Austen*. New York: New York University Press, 1976.

Hardy, John. *Jane Austen's Heroines: Intimacy in Human Relationships*. London: Routledge & Kegan Paul, 1984.

Heath, William, ed. *Discussions of Jane Austen*. Boston: D. C. Heath, 1961.

Hilliard, Raymond F. "*Emma:* Dancing without Space to Turn In." In *Probability, Time, and Space in Eighteenth-Century Literature*, edited by Paula R. Backscheider. New York: AMS Press, 1979.

Kennard, Jean E. *Victims of Convention*. Hamden, Conn.: Archon Books, 1978.

Kestner, Joseph A., III. *Jane Austen: Spatial Structure and Thematic Variations*. Salzburg: Institut für Englischen Sprache und Literatur, University of Salzburg, 1974.

Kirkham, Margaret. *Jane Austen: Feminism and Fiction*. Totowa, N.J.: Barnes & Noble, 1983.

Kissane, James. "Comparison's Blessed Felicity: Character Arrangement in *Emma*." *Studies in the Novel* 2, no. 2 (1970): 173–84.

Knight, Charles A. "Irony and Mr. Knightley." *Studies in the Novel* 2, no. 2 (1970): 185–93.

Kroeber, Karl. *Styles in Fictional Structure: The Art of Jane Austen, Charlotte Brontë, George Eliot*. Princeton: Princeton University Press, 1971.

Lascelles, Mary. *Jane Austen and Her Art*. Oxford: Oxford University Press, 1939.

Lenta, Margaret. "Jane Fairfax and Jane Eyre: Educating Women." *Ariel* 12, no. 4 (1981): 27–41.

Lerner, Laurence. *The Truthtellers: Jane Austen, George Eliot, D. H. Lawrence*. New York: Schocken, 1967.

Liddell, Robert. *Novels of Jane Austen*. London: Longmans, Green, 1963.

Litz, A. Walton. *Jane Austen: A Study of Her Artistic Development*. New York: Oxford University Press, 1965.

Lodge, David, ed. *Jane Austen:* Emma: *A Casebook*. Nashville: Aurora, 1970.

McMaster, Juliet. *Jane Austen on Love*. Victoria, B.C.: University of Victoria, 1978.

———, ed. *Jane Austen's Achievement*. London: Macmillan, 1976.

Mansell, Darrel. *The Novels of Jane Austen: An Interpretation*. London: Macmillan, 1973.

Marshall, Sarah L. "Rationality and Delusion in Jane Austen's *Emma*." *University of Mississippi Studies in English* 9 (1968): 57–67.

Merrett, Robert James. "The Concept of Mind in *Emma*." *English Studies in Canada* 6 (1980): 39–55.

Mews, Hazel. *Frail Vessels: Woman's Role in Women's Novels from Fanny Burney to George Eliot*. London: Athlone, 1969.

Moler, Kenneth L. *Jane Austen's Art of Illusion*. Lincoln: University of Nebraska Press, 1968.

Monaghan, David. *Jane Austen: Structure and Social Vision*. London: Macmillan, 1980.

———, ed. *Jane Austen in a Social Context*. London: Macmillan, 1981.

Moore, E. Margaret. "Emma and Miss Bates: Early Experiences of Separations and the Theme of Dependency in Jane Austen's Novels." *Studies in English Literature 1500–1900* 9 (1969): 573–85.

Morgan, Alice. "On Teaching *Emma*." *Journal of General Education* 24 (1972): 103–8.

Mudrick, Marvin. *Jane Austen: Irony as Defense and Discovery*. Princeton: Princeton University Press, 1952.

Nardin, Jane. *Those Elegant Decorums: The Concept of Propriety in Jane Austen's Novels*. Albany: State University of New York Press, 1973.

Newton, Judith Lowder. *Women, Power, and Subversion: Social Strategies in British Fiction, 1778–1860*. Athens: University of Georgia Press, 1981.

Nineteenth-Century Fiction 30, no. 3 (December 1975). Special Jane Austen issue.

Odmark, John. *An Understanding of Jane Austen's Novels*. Oxford: Basil Blackwell, 1972.

O'Neill, Judith. *Critics on Jane Austen*. Miami: University of Miami Press, 1970.

Page, Norman. *The Language of Jane Austen*. Oxford: Basil Blackwell, 1972.

Paris, Bernard. *Character and Conflict in Jane Austen's Novels*. Detroit: Wayne State University Press, 1979.

Parrish, Stephen M. *Jane Austen:* Emma. New York: Norton, 1972.

Persuasions: Journal of the Jane Austen Society of North America, 1979–.

Phillips, K. C. *Jane Austen's English*. London: Andre Deutsch, 1970.

Piggott, Patrick. *The Innocent Diversion: A Study of Music in the Life and Writings of Jane Austen*. London: Douglas Cleverdon, 1979.

Polhemus, Robert. *Comic Faith: The Great Tradition from Austen to Joyce*. Chicago: University of Chicago Press, 1980.

Poovey, Mary. *The Proper Lady and the Woman Writer: Ideology as Style in the Works of Mary Wollstonecraft, Mary Shelley, and Jane Austen*. Chicago: University of Chicago Press, 1984.

Rees, Joan. *Jane Austen: Woman and Writer*. New York: St. Martin's, 1976.

Roberts, Warren. *Jane Austen and the French Revolution*. New York: St. Martin's, 1979.

Ross, Mary Beth. "Jane Austen as a Political Novelist: Class Consciousness in *Emma*." *The Mary Wollstonecraft Newsletter* 1, no. 1 (1972): 8–12.

Roth, Barry, and Joel Weinsheimer, eds. *An Annotated Bibliography of Jane Austen Studies, 1952–1972*. Charlottesville: University Press of Virginia, 1973.

Scott, P. J. M. *Jane Austen: A Reassessment*. Totowa, N.J.: Barnes & Noble, 1982.

Sherry, Norman. *Jane Austen*. London: Evans Brothers, 1966.

Siefert, Susan. *The Dilemma of the Talented Heroine: A Study in Nineteenth-Century Fiction*. Montreal: Eden Press, 1977.

Smith, LeRoy W. *Jane Austen and the Drama of Woman*. London: Macmillan, 1983.

Southam, B. C. *Jane Austen*. Essex: Longman Group, 1975.

———, ed. *Critical Essays on Jane Austen*. London: Routledge & Kegan Paul, 1968.

———, ed. *Jane Austen: The Critical Heritage*. London: Routledge & Kegan Paul, 1968.

Steeves, Harrison. *Before Jane Austen*. New York: Holt, Rinehart & Winston, 1965.

Studies in the Novel 7, no. 1 (1975). Special Jane Austen issue.

Tamm, Merike. "Performing Heroinism in Austen's *Sense and Sensibility* and *Emma*."

Papers on Language and Literature 15 (1979): 396–407.

Tave, Stuart M. *Some Words of Jane Austen*. Chicago: University of Chicago Press, 1973.

Taylor, Mary Vaiana. "The Grammar of Conduct: Speech Act Theory and the Education of Emma Woodhouse." *Style* 12 (1978): 357–71.

Ten Harmsel, Henrietta. *Jane Austen: A Study in Fictional Conventions*. The Hague: Mouton, 1964.

Todd, Janet, ed. *Jane Austen: New Perspectives*. Women & Literature Series, n.s. 3. New York: Holmes & Meier, 1983.

Watson, J. R. "Mr. Perry's Patients: A View of *Emma*." *Essays in Criticism* 20 (1970): 334–43.

Watt, Ian. *Jane Austen: A Collection of Critical Essays*. Englewood Cliffs, N.J.: Prentice-Hall, 1963.

Weinsheimer, Joel. "Theory of Character: *Emma*." *Poetics Today* 1, nos. 1–2 (1979): 185–211.

———, ed. *Jane Austen Today*. Athens: University of Georgia Press, 1975.

Welty, Eudora. "A Note on Jane Austen." *Shenandoah* 20, no. 3 (1969): 3–17.

Wiesenfarth, Joseph. *The Errand of Form*. New York: Fordham University Press, 1967.

Wilson, Mona. *Jane Austen and Some Contemporaries*. London: Cresset Press, 1938.

Wilt, Judith. "Jane Austen's Men: Inside/Outside 'the Mystery.'" *Women & Literature* 2 (1982): 59–76.

The Wordsworth Circle 7, no. 4 (1976). Special Jane Austen issue.

Wright, Andrew. *Jane Austen's Novels: A Study in Structure*. New York: Oxford University Press, 1953.

Acknowledgments

"The Imagination of Emma Woodhouse" by Stuart M. Tave from *Some Words of Jane Austen* by Stuart M. Tave, © 1973 by The University of Chicago. Reprinted by permission of The University of Chicago Press.

"The Closure of *Emma*" by John Hagan from *Studies in English Literature 1500–1900* 15, no. 4 (Autumn 1975), © 1975 by William Marsh Rice University. Reprinted by permission.

"Love: Surface and Subsurface" (originally entitled "Surface and Subsurface") by Juliet McMaster from *Jane Austen on Love* (Victoria: English Literary Studies), © 1978 by Juliet McMaster. Reprinted by permission of English Literary Studies and the author. This essay first appeared in *Ariel* 5, no. 2 (1974), © 1974 by the Board of Governors, University of Calgary.

"Civilization and the Contentment of *Emma*" by Julia Prewitt Brown from *Jane Austen's Novels: Social Change and Literary Form* by Julia Prewitt Brown, © 1979 by the President and Fellows of Harvard College. Reprinted by permission of Harvard University Press.

"*Emma* and the Charms of Imagination" by Susan Morgan from *In the Meantime: Character and Perception in Jane Austen's Fiction* by Susan Morgan, © 1980 by The University of Chicago. Reprinted by permission of The University of Chicago Press.

"The Importance of Being Frank" by John Peter Rumrich from *Essays in Literature* 8, no. 1 (Spring 1981), © 1981 by Western Illinois University. Reprinted by permission of *Essays in Literature*, Western Illinois University.

"A Comedy of Intimacy" (originally entitled "Conclusion: The Later Novels") by Jan Fergus from *Jane Austen and the Didactic Novel*: Northanger Abbey, Sense and Sensibility, *and* Pride and Prejudice by Jan Fergus, © 1983 by Jan Fergus. Reprinted by permission of Barnes and Noble Books and Macmillan Press Ltd.

"Gossip" (originally entitled "The Talent of Ready Utterance") by Patricia Meyer Spacks from *Gossip* by Patricia Meyer Spacks, © 1985 by Patricia Meyer Spacks. Reprinted by permission of Alfred A. Knopf, Inc.

"Reading Characters: Self, Society, and Text in *Emma*" by Joseph Litvak from *PMLA* 100, no. 5 (October 1985), © 1985 by the Modern Language Association of America. Reprinted by permission of the Modern Language Association of America.

Index

VIVA Modern Critical Interpretations

Available Titles in the Series

Viva

Alice's Adventures in Wonderland

9788130906362 Rs. 145

Animal Farm

9788130906355 In Print

As You Like It

9788130918723 Rs. 195

The Adventures of Huckleberry Finn

9788130907390 Rs. 165

Beowulf

9788130907406 In Print

Beloved

9788130918884 Rs. 195

Black Boy

9788130906737 Rs. 125

Brave New World

9788130906348 In Print

Cat on a Hot Tin Roof

9788130906393 Rs. 99

VIVA Modern Critical Interpretations

Available Titles in the Series

Crime and Punishment

9788130906409 Rs. 175

The Chronicles of Narnia

9788130907468 Rs. 145

The Crucible

9788130906416 Rs. 125

Darkness at Noon

9788130906423 Rs. 145

David Copperfield

9788130918730 Rs. 145

The Death of Artemio Cruz

9788130907475 Rs. 145

Death of a Salesman

9788130906744 Rs. 125

The Divine Comedy

9788130918846 Rs. 175

Don Quixote

9788130904658 Rs. 125

VIVA Modern Critical Interpretations

Available Titles in the Series

Viva

Dracula

9788130906430 Rs. 195

Emerson's Essays

9788130906577 Rs. 175

Emma

9788130918839 Rs. 165

A Farewell to Arms

9788130918754 Rs. 175

Frankenstein

9788130907413 Rs. 145

The General Prologue to the Canterbury Tales

9788130918747 Rs. 175

The Glass Menagerie

9788130907482 In Print

The Grapes of Wrath

9788130906751 Rs. 145

Great Expectations

9788130904597 Rs. 175

VIVA Modern Critical Interpretations

Available Titles in the Series

Viva

The Great Gatsby

9788130906454 Rs. 145

Gulliver's Travels

9788130906461 Rs. 195

Hamlet

9788130918877 Rs. 165

The Iliad

9788130907895 Rs. 145

Invisible Man

9788130906485 In Print

Heart of Darkness

9788130918815 Rs. 165

Jane Eyre

9788130918860 Rs. 195

Julius Caesar

9788130906492 Rs. 125

King Lear

9788130918853 Rs. 165

VIVA Modern Critical Interpretations

Available Titles in the Series

Viva

Long Day's Journey into Night

9788130904634 Rs. 99

Lord of the Flies

9788130904603 Rs. 145

The Lord of the Rings

9788130907956 Rs. 145

The Man without Qualities

9788130907499 Rs. 145

The Merchand of Venice

9788130906522 In Print

Macbeth

9788130906515 Rs. 125

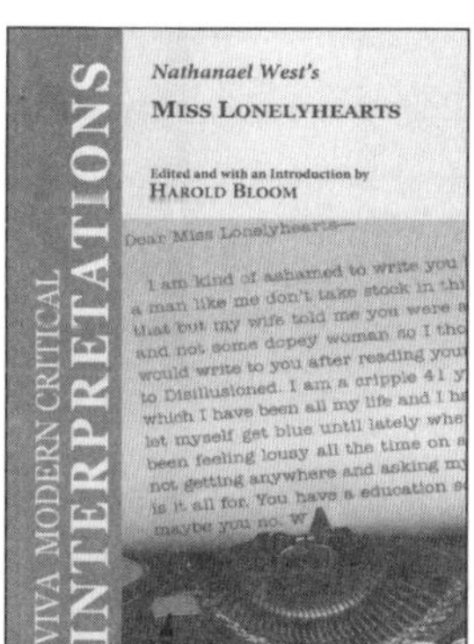

Miss Lonelyhearts

9788130907437 Rs. 125

A Midsummer Night's Dream

9788130918914 Rs. 165

The Metamorphosis

9788130904573 Rs. 99

VIVA Modern Critical Interpretations

Available Titles in the Series

Moby-Dick

9788130906546 Rs. 165

Oedipus

9788130906768 Rs. 165

One Flew Over the Cuckoo's Nest

9788130907444 Rs. 125

One Hundred Years of Solitude

9788130907451 In Print

The Old Man and the Sea

9788130906553 Rs. 125

Othello

9788130918891 Rs. 165

Paradise Lost

9788130906560 In Print

The Pardoner's Tale

9788130904665 Rs. 125

A Passage to India

9788130906584 Rs. 145

VIVA Modern Critical Interpretations

Available Titles in the Series

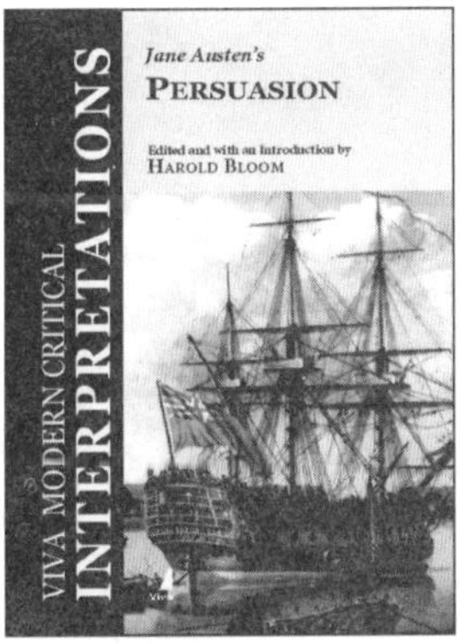

Persuasion

9788130906591 Rs. 175

Pride and Prejudice

9788130906607 Rs. 195

The Red Badge of Courage

9788130906614 Rs. 145

Romeo and Juliet

9788130906621 In Print

The Rubaiyat of Omar Khayyam

9788130904641 Rs. 145

The Scarlet Letter

9788130907505 Rs. 175

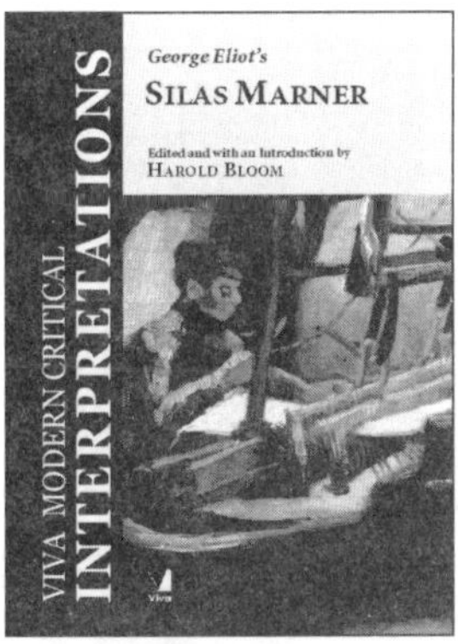

Silas Marner

9788130906638 Rs. 125

Song of Solomon

9788130906645 Rs. 145

Sophie's Choice

9788130906652 Rs. 175

VIVA Modern Critical Interpretations

Available Titles in the Series

The Sound and The Fury

9788130906676 Rs. 195

A Streetcar Named Desire

9788130918716 Rs. 145

Sonnets

9788130918907 Rs. 165

A Tale of Two Cities

9788130906683 Rs. 145

The Tempest

9788130918822 Rs. 175

To Kill a Mockingbird

9788130906775 Rs. 125

Waiting for Godot

9788130906706 Rs. 99

Ulysses

9788130906690 Rs. 145

The Waste Land

9788130904689 Rs. 175

Wuthering Heights

9788130906713 Rs. 175

Young Goodman Brown

9788130906720 Rs. 125